"*In the hope of later solving the cryptogram, Blake bore off the volume in his coat pocket. Many of the great tomes on the shelves fascinated him unutterably, and he felt tempted to borrow them at some later time.*"

—H.P. Lovecraft,
"The Haunter of the Dark"

For Sheila:

Literature lover,
Lovecraft skeptic

TOUR DE LOVECRAFT
- THE TALES -

BY KENNETH HITE

Tour de Lovecraft: The Tales is published by Atomic Overmind Press, in association with Ronin Arts.

Book Layout and Design by Hal Mangold

Cover by Hal Mangold and Kenneth Hite

Interior illustrations by Toren "Macbin" Atkinson

Tour de Lovecraft: The Tales is © 2008 by Kenneth Hite. All rights reserved. Please don't pirate this book, or the Terrible Old Man will be Terribly Upset.

Any discussion of trademarked, service marked, or copyrighted material or entities in this book should not be construed as a challenge to their legal owners. The owners of these trademarks, service marks, and copyrights have not authorized or endorsed this book.

Reproduction of material from within this book for any purposes, by photographic, digital, or other methods of electronic storage and retrieval, is prohibited.

Please address questions and comments concerning this book, as well as requests for notices of new publications, by mail to:

ATOMIC OVERMIND PRESS
143 Wesmond Dr.
Alexandria, VA 22305

Visit us online at **www.atomicovermind.com**.

10 9 8 7 6 5 4 3 2 1

Stock number AOP1001, August 2008.

ISBN 10: 0-9816792-0-X
ISBN 13: 978-0-9816792-0-4

Printed in the United States.

Contents

Foreword i
Introduction iv
A Brief Survey of Lovecraftian Criticism vii
The Stories 1

    The Tomb 1
    Dagon 2
    Polaris 5
    Beyond the Wall of Sleep 6
    The White Ship 7
    The Doom That Came to Sarnath 8
    The Statement of Randolph Carter 11
    The Terrible Old Man 12
    The Tree 13
    Facts Concerning the Late Arthur Jermyn and His Family ... 15
    The Cats of Ulthar 18
    The Temple 21
    Celephaïs 22
    Nyarlathotep 23
    From Beyond 24
    The Picture in the House 26
    The Nameless City 28
    The Quest of Iranon 29
    The Moon-Bog 31
    The Outsider 32
    The Other Gods 34
    Herbert West—Reanimator 35
    The Music of Erich Zann 36
    Hypnos 37
    The Hound 39

THE LURKING FEAR	40
THE RATS IN THE WALLS	42
THE UNNAMABLE	44
THE FESTIVAL	45
UNDER THE PYRAMIDS	46
THE SHUNNED HOUSE	49
THE HORROR AT RED HOOK	51
HE	54
IN THE VAULT	56
COOL AIR	57
THE CALL OF CTHULHU	59
PICKMAN'S MODEL	62
THE STRANGE HIGH HOUSE IN THE MIST	63
THE DREAM-QUEST OF UNKNOWN KADATH	65
THE SILVER KEY	67
THE CASE OF CHARLES DEXTER WARD	69
THE COLOUR OUT OF SPACE	71
THE DUNWICH HORROR	73
THE WHISPERER IN DARKNESS	79
AT THE MOUNTAINS OF MADNESS	80
THE SHADOW OVER INNSMOUTH	84
THE DREAMS IN THE WITCH HOUSE	86
THROUGH THE GATES OF THE SILVER KEY	89
THE THING ON THE DOORSTEP	93
THE SHADOW OUT OF TIME	95
THE HAUNTER OF THE DARK	97
CONCLUSION	101
SOURCES AND RESOURCES	103
INDEX OF LOVECRAFT TALES	107
ABOUT THE AUTHOR	108

Foreword

John Scott Tynes

Like many admirers, I first encountered Lovecraft's work as a teenager. I read "The Colour Out of Space" aloud to my Boy Scout troop on a campout, having found it in my parents' library. From there I descended steadily into a lightless void of obsession and shortly before my twentieth birthday I found myself devoured by a Lovecraftian beast known as Pagan Publishing, a small press I founded and ran for the next twelve years. In those years I dwelled nearer to the epicenter of Lovecraft fandom than is perhaps healthy, but the creative and personal rewards were great -- which is not to say that I escaped the same tradition of shabby-genteel starvation embodied by good old HPL.

During that period, I made several pilgrimages to Providence, Rhode Island, for the NecronomiCon convention. On one of these trips I set out from the hotel on foot and walked the two and a half miles to Swan Point Cemetery, where Lovecraft is buried. I arrived shortly before midnight on August 19th, the eve of his birthday, bearing nothing but a hand-drawn map of the cemetery and a cigarette lighter, which I could only keep lit for a few moments before the heat against my thumb became unbearable. I crept into the moonlit cemetery, mindful of dogs and night watchmen alike, and with the occasional flash of flame I navigated my way through the headstones until I found the Philips family plot. There lay the humble stone reading "I AM PROVIDENCE," lain only in recent years, that marked the final transition of H.P. Lovecraft.

We had a conversation that night, HPL and I, as I sat before his tombstone. Admittedly it was a rather one-sided dialogue, but he seemed game (if quiet) and I had plenty to say. Midnight came and went, I wished him a happy birthday, and then this nocturnal Tour de Lovecraft came to an end.

I wish I could speak of what we spoke, but some sorceries are best left silent. Light illuminates everything but shadows, and those it simply destroys. I believe the world is a better place with mysteries left in it.

Ken Hite is that rarity, a source of illumination that shines upon the shadows and makes them darker: an inverted trapezohedron, perhaps, the anti-antiprism. As a source of information he is delightfully unreliable. Fact, rumor, supposition, and outright bunk all bubble and boil in his creative cauldron and exude a miasma of the unknown. A discussion of Schroedinger's Cat with Ken is likely to lead to conjecture as to whether the fabled chess-playing automaton known as the Turk might well have been operated by Lewis Carroll's Cheshire feline, a line of enquiry not altogether obvious yet somehow weirdly resonant. All of this, of course, makes him an exemplary tour guide, for that is a profession built upon a scaffold of hokum.

There have been three Tours de Hite in my life.

One summer I stayed with Ken and his wife Sheila in Chicago. Ken led me through the city, illuminating his favorite examples of architecture, mysticism, and their many children. Chicago is really Ken's London, his great metropolis of the west. In the way that Tolkien was driven to create a mythology for the land he loved, weaving it together from bits of dead languages and obscure folklore, so too has Ken ensorcelled Chicago and given it a mythic resonance few could perceive unaided. At times his eyes gleam with a messianic fervor and you know the little gray cells of his mind are hard at work preparing their next unwholesome discourse. Of course, like Nyarlathotep come out of Egypt, all Ken's narratives run towards apocalypse.

On another occasion, Ken visited me in Memphis at my ancestral home so I could return the favor. Chicago, it may be said, has no king but rather a succession of princes. Memphis has no such lack. Its king lies in eternal repose at Graceland, not dead but dreaming, awaiting the day when he and JFK and Marilyn and all the other gods of America burst forth from our hearts and reassert themselves in the firmament. We visited Graceland 2, the mystically antipodal reincarnation of Elvis's playland as the home of a father-and-son team of Elvis impersonators and idolaters. Sphinx-like, they riddle visitors but make no sense. Ken and I roamed the city and the surrounding environs, conjugating insanity and paranoia as we went. It was somehow comforting to be on my territory rather than his, but then Ken brings his mental landscape with him everywhere he goes and it tends to subsume the unwary.

For our third tour, neither of us was the guide. Like Harley Warren and Randolph Carter, we set forth in search of dark knowledge in the city of Las Vegas. Everywhere we were surrounded by mystic correspondences and haunting symbols. Cultural, religious, and mythic archetypes loomed large in neon and the psychic weight of all that soul-detritus drove us to drink. Or perhaps it was the other way around.

Which brings us to Ken's latest tour, a genial ramble through the Lovecraft canon. I followed the original publication of these dispatches on his website with interest, as the prospect of Ken turning his strange illumination upon the corpus was too delightful to resist. My attention was rewarded, as will be yours, with his many insights, associations, and criticisms of these familiar tales. Because Ken is first and foremost a creative writer, and not a critic or scholar, he brings to his discursion the camaraderie of a fellow traveler. Other critics, preoccupied with Lovecraft in his historical, psychological, and social contexts, tend to read the stories as some combination of autobiography and existential diatribe. Ken's creative sympathies mean he can speak to Lovecraft as an imaginative craftsman who wielded plot, symbol, theme, and character in the service of his art. Authors tend to make indifferent critics, as they are temperamentally inclined towards the brief but cutting pronouncement rather than the sustained critique. This makes Ken's observations particularly welcome.

I have greatly enjoyed all my tours with Ken and look forward to more. For now, however, let us turn the aged page and see what charnel mysteries await us within.

Bring your cigarette lighter. Ken's supplied the map.

Introduction

I was celebrating my coming of age by a tour of New England—sightseeing, antiquarian, and genealogical—and had planned to go directly from ancient Newburyport to Arkham, whence my mother's family was derived.

—H.P. Lovecraft, "The Shadow Over Innsmouth"

Welcome to the *Tour de Lovecraft: The Tales*. This book is pretty much what that title conveys, a tour through all fifty-one of H.P. Lovecraft's mature works of prose fiction. We're skipping the poetry, the collaborations and ghost-writing and revisions (except for "Through the Gates of the Silver Key"), the travel writing, the artistic and literary criticism and all the other things Lovecraft wrote instead of horror stories. It is my contention that the tale's the thing, and although some of Lovecraft's other works are interesting or fun or valuable, they're not what any of us really signed up for. Like most tours, we'll stay a little longer at the good spots, and try our best to hustle past the weedy, overgrown patches. Hopefully I can point out one or two scenic overlooks along the way, letting you perhaps see some familiar landscape from an angle you hadn't noticed before.

Should you not immediately be familiar with the work of H.P. Lovecraft, it is the general consensus among everyone whose opinion need be listened to that HPL (as we call him on occasion) was the most important and influential horror writer of the twentieth century. The consensus is only slightly less overwhelming that Lovecraft was the second-greatest horror writer in American letters, the first being (of course) Edgar Allan Poe. Not all of Lovecraft's tales are great, though. (Not all of Shakespeare's plays are keepers either, frankly. *Timon of Athens*? *Henry VI, Part III*? Pfah.) More damage has been done to Lovecraft's reputation by the ill-considered overprinting of his lesser works than by almost any other factor. Even the vaunted Library of America ("publishing, and keeping in print, authoritative editions of America's best and most significant writing") decided to present Lovecraft from a historical, rather than an aesthetic, perspective, a decision that preserves on acid-free paper and between sewn bindings such malarkey as "Herbert West—Reanimator," the weak and predictable "Thing on the Doorstep," and Lovecraft's most overrated tale, "The Outsider." This decision, a consequence of the general trend of Lovecraft scholarship and criticism over the last thirty-odd years, doesn't make the life of even we amateur Lovecraft critics any easier.

What, you may then ask, are the great works? In my considered opinion, Lovecraft's reputation can rest on seventeen tales:

Absolutely Perfect: "The Colour Out of Space"
Vanishingly Close To Perfect: *The Case of Charles Dexter Ward*, "The Call of Cthulhu," *At the Mountains of Madness*, "The Dunwich Horror," "The Shadow Over Innsmouth"
Masterpieces: "The Whisperer in Darkness," "The Rats in the Walls", "The Music of Erich Zann"
Great: "The Dreams in the Witch House," "The Haunter of the Dark," "Pickman's Model," "The Shunned House," "The Shadow Out of Time," "The Strange High House in the Mist," "The Doom That Came to Sarnath," "The Cats of Ulthar"

The rest are not great, although some of them are quite enjoyable.

Whether any of this makes Lovecraft "literature" is a question rather more fraught, and one we don't really have space for. But that said, Lovecraft has been, and can be, read critically and analytically. Every so often in this Tour, we do that, amid the general ruck of aimless commentary.

Which leads me, elliptically, to the question of how this Tour came about in the first place. Every winter in my LiveJournal,[1] I do a little

---

1. At **http://princeofcairo.livejournal.com** should you be interested, and feel free to drop by if you are.

devoted long-form serial, usually an entry a day (or as close as I can get) on a specific topic. From March 2 to June 27, 2007, I posted one entry on each story included in the three recent Penguin Classics Lovecraft anthologies edited by S.T. Joshi, in their table of contents order, calling it the "Tour de Lovecraft." Over the course of that Tour, I received a number of gratifying comments asking if I planned to collect the Tour into a single volume.[2] After enough such had built up, I decided to go ahead and do that.

For this publication, I re-ordered the Tour to set the tales in the order that Lovecraft wrote them, and tweaked the text of the entries to reflect that decision. I occasionally pulled clever things I said in the individual entries' comment threads up into the main text where they deserved it. Sometimes I said those things in response to quite clever remarks from my readers. I have tried to indicate other people's ideas where I could, but the pseudonymous nature of LiveJournal, and the exigencies of clear writing, mean that I might not have been able to do so. If I have lifted your thoughts, I hope you'll forgive me, or at least take comfort in the notion that I've also stolen a great deal from George Wetzel, Northrop Frye, S.T. Joshi, and Peter Cannon, among other critical heavyweights.

I also polished up the prose somewhat, although it retains the vulgar glister of its informal beginnings rather more than my usual work does. And finally, to give people who loyally read the whole thing for free in my LiveJournal a reason to feel like they should buy this compilation, I added a few thousand words of additional insight, commentary, and thought that occurred to me as I went through and copy-edited the text. Finally, to help put this amateur, not to say haphazard, effort at Lovecraftian criticism into some sort of context, I wrote "A Brief Survey of Lovecraftian Criticism," which immediately follows this Introduction.

---

2. I also received an invitation from an editor at *Weird Tales* to present a similar Tour in those hallowed pages; should that proceed as intended, we may return to this well for *Tour de Lovecraft 2: The Settings* in about a year from now.

A Brief Survey of Lovecraftian Criticism

Literary criticism and H.P. Lovecraft both get a bad rap, often the same one: "Useless tail-chasing with no relevance to real human responses and nothing to contribute to the understanding of literature; the obsession of people not capable of dealing honestly with art as it is." Ironically, this identical libel is leveled by Lovecraft fans at literary critics, and by literary critics at Lovecraft and his fans. Both should know better, not least because H.P. Lovecraft was a literary critic of rare perception and talent. Attempting to address the literature (and theory) of the weird without Lovecraft's *Supernatural Horror in Literature* would be almost as bootless as attempting to do so without discussing Poe's critical work. But Lovecraft fans see literary critics, especially academic critics, as effete snobs who dismiss genre fiction—especially supernatural horror—as worthless trash for no better reason than sheer bigotry and laziness. And literary critics can be forgiven for looking at the sheer morass of truly terrible genre fiction and deciding that their time is better spent reading Hawthorne, and Poe, and Melville, especially when genre fans show little or no understanding of those authors, or of why they are all considerably greater than H.P. Lovecraft.

The seeds of the problem were sown early, with Lovecraft's failure to sell an anthology of weird stories to a real publisher. His work, mired as it was among the Seabury Quinn and Nictzin Dyalhis garbage, hackily type-set between lurid Margaret Brundage covers, never really made it onto the radar of American literary culture, despite the appearance of "The Colour Out of Space" on the "Roll of Honor" in Edward J. O'Brien's influential *Best Short Stories* anthology. After Lovecraft's death, his work was left in the hands of three worshipful fans: Robert H. Barlow, Donald Wandrei, and August Derleth, which rapidly reduced (following feuds and wartime service) to essentially Derleth alone. Derleth's insistence on publishing every word of Lovecraft's writing (including his awful juvenilia, as well as mediocrities like "Herbert West—Reanimator"), larding the anthologies with memorials and tributes by still less-famous names, and generally treating the entire enterprise as a combination religious cult and high-school reunion led to Edmund Wilson, the dean of American literary critics, writing in "Tales of the Marvellous and the Ridiculous" (1945) that "the Lovecraft cult, I fear, is on even a more infantile level than the Baker Street Irregulars and the cult of Sherlock Holmes." For many years, Wilson's was the last word by a "real critic" on the subject of H.P. Lovecraft.

August Derleth was an excellent writer in his own field, regional fiction, and an occasionally gifted pasticheur. His Lovecraft pastiches—especially the "posthumous collaborations," which consisted of Derleth writing a story based on a Lovecraftian commonplace-book entry—are not his best, however. Derleth also read Lovecraft's cosmic horror in the light of his own Roman Catholicism, not merely establishing a Pythagorean "elemental" scheme for Lovecraft's various entities (harmless enough) but adding a pantheon of "good" Elder Gods and recasting the blind, Darwinian universe of Azathoth and others into a Manichean struggle of good and evil. As the publisher and editor of Arkham House, Derleth published and encouraged "Lovecraftian" fiction that adopted his understanding of the Mythos, and even when he published stories in a less dualistic vein he often included in the anthologies a totalizing essay setting out his own vision as Lovecraft's. (This lamentable trend did not die with Derleth.) All that said, of course, Derleth was, at least, keeping Lovecraft in print, seeding his tales into other publishers' anthologies, and building a stable of writers dedicated to their own vision of Lovecraft's work. Derleth also underwrote the publication of five volumes of Lovecraft's letters, ensuring that future critics would have plenty of ammunition with which to snottily condescend to Derleth's misunderstanding of Lovecraft's philosophy. In short, without August Derleth, H.P. Lovecraft might well be no more famous today than William Hope Hodgson—who owes some large part of his small fame to the fact that Lovecraft's literary criticism mentions him.

August Derleth also published the single best, most important literary-critical study of H.P. Lovecraft to date, Fritz Leiber's "A Literary Copernicus" (1949). Leiber, soon to be a major talent not just in horror, but in fantasy and science fiction as well, understood that Lovecraft partook of all those traditions, especially science fiction. Leiber wrote that Lovecraft "shifted the focus of supernatural dread from man and his little world and his gods, to the stars and the black and unplumbed gulfs of intergalactic space." Like Leiber, many of the increasingly confident and important SF and fantasy authors of the postwar era recognized Lovecraft for his impact, even if, unlike Leiber, they (mainly devotees of manly, modernist prose a la Heinlein and Hemingway) denigrated his actual writing. The SF community, like Lovecraft fandom, found itself marginalized by the academy, and developed its own pet critics and scholars, often coming (in the great tradition of Dryden, Pope, Coleridge, Poe, Swinburne, Eliot, Auden, and Lovecraft) from the ranks of successful authors.

Among them were the two most significant figures in Lovecraftian criticism in the 1960s and 1970s, friends and collaborators L. Sprague de Camp and Lin Carter. Carter, a pasticheur of even more limited gifts than Derleth, became a (quite skilled) editor at Ballantine Books in 1969. In the wake of the Tolkien boom, he drove the reprinting not only of Lovecraft but of Clark Ashton Smith, William Hope Hodgson, Lord Dunsany, William Beckford, Arthur Machen, and other key figures who influenced Lovecraft. Carter also churned out numerous anthologies (and a very able history of fantasy, *Imaginary Worlds*) tying Lovecraft and the Cthulhu Mythos to the burgeoning fantasy scene, a tack he followed in his literary biography *Lovecraft: A Look Behind the Cthulhu Mythos*. Perhaps thanks to his strong fantasy leanings, Carter was sympathetic to Derleth's interpretation of the Mythos. With de Camp, Carter edited, revised, and expurgated Robert E. Howard's fiction for Lancer Books, further expanding the reputation of the "Lovecraft Circle." In 1975, de Camp published the first full-length biography of Lovecraft, *Lovecraft: A Biography*. Although thoroughly researched and quite well-written, it has been criticized for making Lovecraft seem a pathetic figure, along with a helping of armchair psychoanalysis and a perceived over-emphasis on Lovecraft's racism. In part to counter de Camp's work, Frank Belknap Long published a windy reminiscence that contributed little to critical or biographical understanding, and Willis Conover edited his and Lovecraft's correspondence into *Lovecraft at Last*, a biography of Lovecraft's last year and his relationship with a young fan (Conover). This work, its influence limited by its small-press distribution, is probably the finest portrait of Lovecraft as a human being, although Conover was obviously working from within a very narrow perspective.

But in the 1970s, armchair psychoanalysis was all the rage. The scholar Barton L. St.-Armand examined "The Rats in the Walls" as an exploration of the Jungian unconscious and *The Case of Charles Dexter Ward* as a novel driven by homesickness. A French critic, Maurice Levy, analyzed Lovecraft's tales as HPL's obsessive subconscious search for a "cure" for his own pessimism, racism, and reactionary aesthetic. (Ever avant-garde, the critic and novelist Colin Wilson had diagnosed Lovecraft as neurotic, even psychotic, and "sick" in *The Strength to Dream* (1961), a study of literary imagination. On the other hand, he treated Lovecraft as a serious writer.) In America, HPL fan and Ph.D. in psychology Dirk Mosig led the way with "The Four Faces of 'The Outsider,'" a full-throated assault on the established New Critical version of HPL that saw him solely (or primarily) as mythographer and genre author. Mosig also expanded on Richard L. Tierney's initial demolition of "The Derleth Mythos" in "H.P. Lovecraft: Myth-Maker," an attempt to divine Lovecraft's metaphysics from his fiction to the detriment of the received Derlethian wisdom. Mosig pioneered the intensive examination of Lovecraft's writings as expressions of Lovecraft that has slowly taken over Lovecraft studies—a revolution made possible and plausible by de Camp's biography, for all that the later critics disparaged it.

One seminal development in Lovecraft criticism in the 1970s demands mention: the publication of Meade and Penny Frierson's fanzine-cum-festschrift *HPL* in 1972. With Stuart David Schiff (who would go on to become one of the horror field's most gifted critics and editors) at the non-fiction editing helm, this 144-page hectographed amateur publication was a depth charge. In addition to plentiful fiction and art, it contained memoirs or criticism by leading scholars, gifted authors, and Lovecraft's correspondents, including Robert Bloch, Fritz Leiber, Joseph Payne Brennan, E. Hoffmann Price, Colin Wilson, and James Wade. The two most significant works within were Richard Tierney's aforementioned de-Derlethification "The Derleth Mythos," and "The Cthulhu Mythos" by George T. Wetzel. This revision of Wetzel's landmark article from 1955 (during the last echoes of the post-mortem "Lovecraft circle" critical scene) remains almost the only serious attempt at a structuralist analysis of Lovecraft's fictional oeuvre. (Indeed, it approaches archetypal criticism a la Northrop Frye.) To paraphrase Brian Eno on the Velvet Underground, *HPL* only sold 500 copies, but everyone who bought one started writing Lovecraft criticism, including Dirk Mosig.

Another was Dirk Mosig's protégé, an Indiana prodigy named S.T. Joshi. While still in high school, Joshi contracted with Kent State University Press to produce a bibliography of Lovecraft. While at Brown University, he produced a landmark anthology, *H.P. Lovecraft: Four Decades of Criticism*, the first book on Lovecraft from an academic press (Ohio University Press). Although it reprinted Wetzel's study, it further aimed critical thought in the direction of Lovecraft's influences, metaphysics, and philosophy. (A second, centennial, anthology edited with David E. Schultz, *An Epicure in the Terrible* (1991), included more thematic material, albeit still in service to Lovecraft the metaphysician.) In 1979 he also started *Lovecraft Studies*, a journal for the academic discussion of HPL, which provided an outlet for gifted scholars such as Steven J. Mariconda, Peter Cannon,[3] and pulp historian Will Murray. He further labored to produce critical, error-free texts of Lovecraft's work, helming the revised editions

---

3. In this survey, I have unfairly slighted Peter Cannon, who shares Price's (and Lovecraft's) sense of humor and Joshi's rigor, and whose 1981 *Lovecraft Studies* essay "Sunset Terrace Imagery in Lovecraft" is a key work for a symbolist reading of HPL.

at August Derleth's old company, Arkham House. Truly the Bastille had fallen, as Joshi was firmly in the Tierney-Mosig "anti-Derleth" school of Puritan neo-orthodoxy. Over the next decade, as *Lovecraft Studies* flourished, and the revised Lovecraft texts became available (1984-1989), S.T. Joshi was the overwhelmingly dominant force in Lovecraft scholarship and Lovecraft criticism.

Lovecraft studies (and *Lovecraft Studies*) suffered with the rest of the academy from the "French Disease" in the 1990s, ushered in by Donald Burleson's deconstructionist Lovecraft study, *Disturbing the Universe* (1990), which was, however, published by an academic press (University of Kentucky). Even the best of scholars fell victim to the bug on occasion, leaving the floor clear for the historicist Joshi and his interpretations. Joshi fiercely emphasized what he saw as the essential unity of Lovecraft's vision, as expressed in the fiction, the letters, and the critical essays. For Joshi, Lovecraft is most valuable as a philosopher, an exponent of the unified life, a tireless evangelist for the gospel of atheist cosmicism, or what he calls "mechanist materialism." This vision of Lovecraft's vision received full expression in Joshi's magisterial biography, *H.P. Lovecraft: A Life* (1996), probably the most comprehensive one-volume biography possible. Joshi also labored mightily and long to claim the reactionary Lovecraft for the Left, a project cast into some doubt by Michel Houellebecq's 1991 *Lovecraft: Against the World, Against Life*, which made Lovecraft's reaction the source and soul of his horror.

Although I take plenty of shots at Joshi and his interpretations later on in this Tour, I want to make clear that he is the indispensable man at the heart of what academic Lovecraft revival there has been; the August Derleth, if you will, of serious Lovecraft criticism. Like Derleth, he shows an unvarying tendency to read his own views onto HPL, but also like Derleth he does not exclude or punish those who differ. Joshi's *The Weird Tale* (1990) examined Lovecraft in the light of the other great horrorists of the century: Blackwood, Bierce, James, Machen, and Dunsany, providing intensely interesting and valuable insights on them and their great Providence scion. His reading in the literature of the weird is vast, and his historical research (both first-hand in the John Hay Library, and secondhand by identifying problems for other scholars) has made Lovecraft one of the best-documented literary figures in any century.

Joshi's only rival for eminence in the field during the 1980s and 1990s was Robert M. Price, who edited *The Crypt of Cthulhu*, "a pulp magazine and theological journal" perhaps intended to take some of the piss out of the academic tone of *Lovecraft Studies*. A fanzine that reprinted a lot of minor Cthulhiana by various authors, *Crypt* gave Price a leg up as an editor for various small presses, including many, many collections from Chaosium, the publishers of the **Call of Cthulhu** roleplaying game. Like *Crypt*, **CoC** bowed in 1981, and set off its own tsunami of Lovecraft fandom, which eventually washed up in critical studies. (As it did in my case.) Price's anthologies for Chaosium featured a strong historical perspective, tracing individual themes and topoi backward to Victorian fiction and forward through the various waves of "Cthulhu Mythos stories," presenting the tales as serial myths rather than Joshi-style philosophical proofs. Price, a theologian and minister, occasionally toyed with neo-Derlethianism, pointing out that Lovecraft presented his mythologies as mythologies within the fiction, and analyzing them in those terms rather than as variables in mechanist-materialist equations. This has its own delicious irony, as Price's other main contribution to the critical study of HPL is to define all of Lovecraft's gods as aliens, and to describe Lovecraft's mythopoetic project as a "demythologization."

In the new century, scholarship seems to be in something of a hiatus: the Chaosium anthologies have slowed to a crawl, and both *Lovecraft Studies* and *Crypt of Cthulhu* have been sporadic in the last decade. (Joshi published another biography of Lovecraft in 2001, a "biography in letters" called *A Visible Life*, and a very interesting primary research work on *Lovecraft's Library*.) After 70 years Lovecraft seems to have made the jump to cult figure in the academy, however, showing up in works by hip scholars like Erik Davis and Victoria Nelson, and in an increasing number of studies of the currently trendy Gothic. Robert H. Waugh, an English professor at SUNY (New Paltz) has apparently decided to take a swipe at the "reigning scholar" crown with *Monster in the Mirror*, a 2006 anthology of essays centering on "The Outsider" and privileging Lovecraft's anti-Semitism while remaining sympathetic to the work. Joyce Carol Oates in the mainstream, and China Miéville in the spec-fic world, have taken up the mantle of critical Lovecraft defenders. Lovecraft finds himself in both the Library of America and (in a trilogy edited by S.T. Joshi) Penguin Classics; surely, no more imprimatur is needed. But that said, Lovecraft's Library of America appearance spawned a whole new series of ignorant reviews that could have been ground out by a reanimated Edmund Wilson, save that Wilson was a much better writer. Withal, Lovecraft repays critical study; the work is its own reward. If that allows too much fanboy raving, it also leaves air in the room for the interested and intelligent reader, who has only one or two pillars to avoid. (Pity the poor would-be Shakespeare amateur, with tens of thousands of interpretations blotting out the work like so many tentacles.) Like August Derleth's Elder Gods' never-ending battle against the black magic of the Great Old Ones, and like the later critics' never-ending battle against August Derleth, the battle for Lovecraft's critical reputation will perhaps go on until the stars once more come right and great Cthulhu strides forth again.

The Tomb

[June 1917]

We're off!

And with a jolt, we begin with early, prolix, Poe-wannabe Lovecraft. "The Tomb" is essentially *Charles Dexter Ward* before Lovecraft really knew how to write a plot, use setting, or set a mood. Jervas Dudley, though, is surprisingly well developed for an HPL character, and amazing for an early HPL character, possibly because, as Joshi theorizes, he's a thinly disguised version of Lovecraft himself. Fighting your way through the interminable drifts of this story (it almost has more in common with his forgettable juvenilia, for all that it barely predates "Dagon"), you come across a few nuggets of interest, beginning with this early version of Lovecraft's hyperdimensional cosmos:

> *It is an unfortunate fact that the bulk of humanity is too limited in its mental vision to weigh with patience and intelligence those isolated phenomena, seen and felt only by a psychologically sensitive few, which lie outside its common experience. Men of broader intellect know that there is no sharp distinction betwixt the real and the unreal; that all things appear as they do only by virtue of the delicate individual physical and mental media through which we are made conscious of them; but the prosaic materialism of the majority condemns as madness the flashes of super-sight which penetrate the common veil of obvious empiricism.*

I'm also susceptible to the way Lovecraft roots and buttresses his various hateful lineages, and to associated things like the "mumbled tales of the weird rites and godless revels of bygone years in the ancient hall." And this is just a really great line:

"Several faces I recognised; though I should have known them better had they been shrivelled or eaten away by death and decomposition."

Other than that, it's mostly useful as a kind of Burgess Shale of Lovecraft's artistic evolution. Like "Dagon," "The Tomb" introduces a lot of themes and topoi that HPL will return to often—the interpermeability of the real and dream worlds (*Dream-Quest*, the other "Dreamlands" tales, "Dreams in the Witch House"), and of history and the present ("He," "Shadow Out of Time," "Dreams in the Witch House" again), antiquarian tendencies as the road to doom ("He" again, "Whisperer in the Darkness," "Haunter of the Dark," etc.), blasphemous or cursed family lines ("Rats in the Walls," "Lurking Fear," "Dunwich Horror," etc.), and even that cleansing blast of lightning ("Lurking Fear," "Haunter of the Dark"). As I mention above, the whole story, with its neurasthenic, ancestrally-obsessed scion possessed by his villainous forefather, prefigures *Charles Dexter Ward*.

Since it's a sloppier story than "Dagon," it also introduces a lot of things that HPL didn't wind up using so much, beginning with the "dryads" (and the parallel "hideous soul of the forest"), the almost explicit fairy-tale structure (parallelling Theseus' life), buried treasure and necromancy (both surprisingly rare in Lovecraft), and the Georgian rip-roaring attitude exemplified by the drinking song. One can't help but feel, reading this, that there was the seed of a really good Hell-Fire Club novel in HPL somewhere.

DAGON

[JULY 1917]

Like the narrator, Lovecraft saw the central action of "Dagon"—the crawl across the primordial mud flat away from the temple—in a dream.

Even more than "The Tomb," this is an appropriate beginning in so many ways. It's really the first piece of mature fiction Lovecraft wrote (and the first he published in *Weird Tales*), and it introduces a surprisingly developed set of the themes he'd visit for the next 20 years. There's the "archaeological exposition" in the form of hieroglyphics or bas-reliefs, the topos of the submerged evil god/place, the allusions to existing myth but with substantial changes, and even the final despairing narrative shriek to break closure conclusively. If "The Tomb" is *Charles Dexter Ward* in embryo, "Dagon" is both "Call of Cthulhu" and *Mountains of Madness* in ovo. "Dagon" is also the story that forced Lovecraft to begin his lifelong project of defending, and explaining critically, weird fiction. (Members of the APA where he first circulated the tale disliked it, and its genre, intensely.) As great a writer as HPL is, he's almost as great a critic. (This is surprisingly common.)

This story thus begins both those strands of his thought, and is almost the purest exposition (save the prose-poems) of his thesis that weird fiction is built up from incident, not from action. This, perhaps, is why the narrator is such a passive weakling. Indeed, more than most Lovecraft stories, we really are faced with an unreliable narrator. The sunken continent rises while the narrator dreams wildly, and sinks while he is delirious. In short, he enters and leaves Dagon's realm through his dreams (on a boat, like Max in *Where the Wild Things Are*). His only proof is nothing: he clearly remembers seeing Dagon at the temple, and he hears noises…but are you going to believe a self-confessed suicidal morphine addict? This device keeps this story surprisingly fresh; it's one of Lovecraft's few completely successful (in my mind) variations on Poe's structure, and he continues to ring its changes all the way to "The Shadow Out of Time."

****

Lovecraft, obviously, idolized Poe, calling him (incorrectly, but understandably) "my only model" or something to that effect in a quote I can't seem to track down right now. He learned a vast amount from Poe; lessons best summarized by Lovecraft's own enumeration of Poe's virtues as a craftsman:

> *Poe's spectres thus acquired a convincing malignity possessed by none of their predecessors, and established a new standard of realism in the annals of literary horror. The impersonal and artistic intent, moreover, was aided by a scientific attitude not often found before; whereby Poe studied the human mind rather than the usages of Gothic fiction, and worked with an analytical knowledge of terror's true sources which doubled the force of his narratives and emancipated him from all the absurdities inherent in merely conventional shudder-coining... Poe, too, set a fashion in consummate craftsmanship ... we can constantly trace his influence in such things as the maintenance of a single mood and achievement of a single impression in a tale, and the rigorous paring down of incidents to such as have a direct bearing on the plot and will figure prominently in the climax.*

But unlike Poe, HPL is (usually) not really interested in any given human being's psychology. Rather, Lovecraft's heroes, like those of most Gothics, are societal proxies. They are stand-ins for the (shaky) structure of scientific rationality; a sort of mirror-image of the (John W.) Campbellian heroic Everyman, if you will. Lovecraft takes the characteristics of Poe's "haunted man" and projects them onto humanity (and, as in all good Gothics, onto the landscape) stating effectively that there are cosmic truths which we cannot afford to look at, and fundamental limitations that no Faustian drive or scientific irony can overcome, because these limitations are innate in humanity.

It will take Lovecraft a while to figure this out for himself; there are a lot of very tiresome neurasthenic, hysterical narrators to come before he finds his more natural métier in dry, academic madness.

Essentially, then, where Poe was writing psychological horror (of, *naturellement*, a very emotional, Romantic bent), Lovecraft was writing existential horror. As early as "Dagon," you can see it hatch.

Polaris

[May 1918]

It's a shame that "Polaris" is so offputting for so many reasons, from the inanition of the narrator ("I was feeble and given to strange faintings") to the really repugnant racism (Yay "tall, grey-eyed men of Lomar"! Boo "squat, hellish, yellow fiends [who] knew not the scruples of honour"!) to the really repugnant racism ("Inutos" = Inuit). (The whole polar myth is just soaking in racist broth; see Joscelyn Godwin's summary of it in *Arktos*, if you haven't already availed yourself.) The language is florid—what we'd call 'Dunsanian' if Lovecraft hadn't written it a year before he ever read Dunsany. And there's no shortage of supposed-to-be-exciting adjectives.

But it's probably the most philosophically (if not structurally) interesting of these three early Lovecraft tales. Lovecraft wrote it to refute William James (or, rather, to refute a Jamesian friend, Maurice Moe), and the entire point of the tale is that we don't know (nor does the narrator) which is the dream world and which the real world. (Think hard now—do we actually have any more reason to believe in the nameless "house of stone and brick south of a sinister swamp" than in the city of Lomar?) Layered onto that, the story strongly implies that the "dream world" of Lomar is our own world 26,000 years (one full precession of the equinoxes) ago, and hence: that time and consciousness and history are cyclic, that the soul is not individual or even time-bound, and that even today the intellectuals are nodding off on the peaks while our civilization enters its terminal state. Joshi chose wisely when he used this tale and "Shadow Out of Time" to bracket one volume of his Penguin edition—they're almost identical in theme and even in aspects of content.

Lots of reasons to go back to "Polaris," then, and not just because it's where Lovecraft made up—and importantly, made up names for—his first a) ancient civilization, b) alien race (assuming the "Gnophkehs" aren't just cavemen), and c) tome of forgotten lore, in this case, the *Pnakotic Manuscripts*. Plus a much cooler version of the "evil star" motif that he tries out again next, in "Beyond the Wall of Sleep."

Somebody who wanted to recast the entire Mythos as a Spenglerian, neo-Platonist, Gnostic myth-cycle could do worse than build on the frozen foundations of Lomar.

BEYOND THE WALL OF SLEEP

[SPRING 1919]

Aside from its title having inspired a pretty rockin' Smithereens song, this story is not worth much.

I'm normally not one for subversive readings for subversion's sake—evil Sherlock Holmeses and noble Draculas are, if anything, more tiresome and hackneyed nowadays than mere pastiches are—but I've got to say that the only way I can even stand to re-read this story is by casting the "brother of light" as a kind of cousin to the Colour Out of Space. When it starts smarmily assuring Lovecraft's Mary Sue[4] about their noble kinship in the dream-world, or prating about how the poor hillbilly Joe Slater was "unfit to bear the intellect of cosmic entity," I just want to root hard for Algol.

This is HPL at his most condescending, snobby, and faux-genteel, and it grates almost more than the racism, which is almost never at the core of any Lovecraft story, unlike the snide classism he presumes upon in this one. Of course, this was the era when elite, progressive eugenicists were faking research on white "Kallikaks" to support programs of euthanasia and sterilization for the "unfit lower orders," and a lot of those narratives carried racial overtones as well. For example, the "Jukes" were of mixed race, as were the interestingly-named "Slaughters" of upstate New York, who may have been the "Slahters or Slaters" mentioned in the *New York Tribune* article

---

4. A "Mary Sue" is the generic name for the author's idealized self-image, especially when used as a character in fan fiction.

Lovecraft read that helped inspire this story. (Although even here, Lovecraft goes out of his way to avoid a racial angle, describing Joe Slater as devolved "white trash," and mentioning his blue eyes and blond beard.)

Lovecraft used his correspondents in the Catskills, and the historical nova, to some good effect. Also, the thought-radio is neat, and the notion of the separate worlds whose joining is fatal is always a good vein for Lovecraft to work, but even as a rehearsal for "Shadow Out of Time" or "Dreams in the Witch House" this tale is talky and substandard. It's short, though, so that's good.

THE WHITE SHIP

[OCTOBER 1919]

Although the tale obviously prefigures *Dream-Quest*, the later novel will essentially reverse this story's moral. An unexceptionable, if unexceptional, immram, "The White Ship" is the sort of story that just sits there and breathes allegory at you, gravid with Symbolic Freight.

Take your pick:

- The White Ship is the path to Self-Knowledge (Hermetic, Jungian, whatever, take your pick).
- The White Ship is the True Soul, of which we cannot partake.
- The White Ship is Dream.
- The White Ship was sent by the ocean-soul to kidnap Elton; the story is an early sketch for "Shadow Over Innsmouth".
- The White Ship is Jesus; the story is about HPL's regrets at being an atheist.
- The Bird of Heaven is Jesus; the story is about HPL's insistence that religion is hateful illusion meant to lead us away from happiness.

- The White Ship is the illusion of Human Progress; trying to reach Cathuria leads only to watery Cthulhoid destruction.
- The White Ship is the Psychopomp; Basil Elton is a continuously-reincarnate spirit of the Eltons, and the Bearded Man is his Lar, the spirit of his family.
- The Bearded Man is Nyarlathotep, on the grounds that anything problematic in a Lovecraft story always winds up being Nyarlathotep.
- The White Ship is a political allegory for Warren Harding, who evades all the real troublesome issues, tries to maroon you in a land of happy talk, but eventually smashes up when you follow him (West) into splendid isolation and normalcy.
- The White Ship is a political allegory for Woodrow Wilson, who exposes you to horrible dangers, strands you in pointless stagnation while claiming it's for your own good, and wrecks everything when you follow him to Cathuria, which is the League of Nations, and hence impossible of attainment.

See how easy that is?

Me, I think that Darrell Schweitzer has it right and "The White Ship" is Lovecraft playing at allegory, that the message is transparent Epicureanism, and that it's pastiching Dunsany's "Idle Days on the Yann."

THE DOOM THAT CAME TO SARNATH

[DECEMBER 3, 1919]

This is a terrific, terrific story. I've loved it forever. I set part of one of my early **Call of Cthulhu** roleplaying campaigns in Sarnath an unspecified number of years before the DOOM. (Time gates and dream-based time travel, since you asked.) This story is like caramel. I'm sure there are people who don't like caramel, but don't ask me to understand them.

****

One real quick note on the city's name: Sarnath, near Varanasi, is a historical city in India where the Buddha first taught the Dharma. This is almost certainly a coincidence.

Lovecraft thought he made it up, and then he thought he stole the name from Dunsany. He doesn't seem to have known about the actual Sarnath in India at all.

If you ask me, it's what happens when you start with 'Sardathrion' (the paradise city of the gods from Dunsany's "Time and the Gods," upon which this story is pastiched) and blend it with 'Karnak', which is probably what Lovecraft was thinking of given the similarity of the description of Sarnath to that of "hundred-gated Thebes" in Homer.

In support of this completely wild speculation, I'll note that the same blend explains 'Kadatheron,' which also appears in this story.

****

"Sarnath" is one of HPL's three best pre-1926 tales, up there with "The Music of Erich Zann" and "Rats in the Walls." And where "Rats" is his perfect 'Poe' story, this is his perfect 'Dunsany' story. ("Erich Zann" is his perfect 'Lovecraft' story to that point, although with "Call of Cthulhu" HPL goes and rewrites the rulebook for perfect Lovecraft stories.)

Like "Rats," the tone and aim are slightly different than the model. (In this case "Time and the Gods," primarily, but there's lots of others in there.) But like "Rats" (and "Dunwich Horror," his perfect 'Machen' story) the difference is an intentional culinary choice, in this case a surprisingly mature one given the story's early composition—1919! Like I say, HPL writes nothing to touch it for two more years, although "Cats of Ulthar" comes perhaps close.

It's a little denser than Dunsany (a custard, not a meringue). But it makes up for the added weight with both mythic resonance and horror. Dunsany's tales sound like late-Classical myths, something spun up by Virgil or Ovid or one of those guys and translated by an Edwardian Irishman. Lovecraft's best work sounds like early myth, something desperately smooshed together by Hesiod or hinted at by Euripides and translated by a shocked Cotton Mather.[5] And Dunsany only very seldom gets into true horror, although he'll make more small hairs stand up on the back of your neck than any other fantasiste this side of Fritz Leiber.

****

This story is pregnant with Biblical weight, referencing Daniel at Belshazzar's feast, the fate of Dagon before the Ark, and the fate prophesied for Edom in Isaiah.[6] Even the dimensions of Sarnath and the fulsome description of its wonders recall the New Jerusalem in Ezekiel and Revelation. But of course, it's Lovecraft, so the avenging God who brings the well-deserved DOOM to Sarnath is not YHWH but Bokrug, and his angels are demonic ab-human moon-spawn.

****

There's all kinds of other places you could go with this story. I'll toss a little one out here for now, as it suits my own personal urban-mythic obsessions. Consider the Lovecraftian city topos. As with cities in most of the Western literary canon, a city is either Dis (Ib, Irem, New York) or Jerusalem (Sarnath, Providence, Randolph Carter's 'sunset city'). What this story tells us is that Dis and Jerusalem are the same city. Sarnath destroys Ib, Ib destroys Sarnath. We see the same evolution with Kadath and Pnakotus—both locus of horror and alien paradise, the horror of the place occurring precisely because the city was once an alien paradise—and in a

---

[5]. Mather had a fine amateur scientific mind, for 1690; an archaeologist, a naturalist, and to the extent of his abilities quite the natural philosopher. He may have been wrong about witches—and even there his error was more in the realm of legal than scientific theory—but he was right about smallpox inoculation.

[6]. Isaiah 34:12: "They shall name it No Kingdom There, and all its princes shall be nothing." One of the few actual improvements to the poetry of the King James Version made by the RSV. The KJV, normally the gold standard, has this kind of meh line: "They shall call the nobles thereof to the kingdom, but none shall be there, and all her princes shall be nothing." On the other hand, the KJV comes roaring back to kick all kinds of ass in the very next verse: "And thorns shall come up in her palaces, nettles and brambles in the fortresses thereof: and it shall be an habitation of dragons, and a court for owls." I'm a Calvinist; of course I love Isaiah. I'm a writer; of course I love the King James.

twisted way with Innsmouth (a place of horrible exodus becomes a place of welcome pilgrimage) and even R'lyeh, the promised New Jerusalem of the apocalyptic future when the stars come right again.

"The crooked shall be made straight, and the rough ways shall be made smooth." You tell 'em, Isaiah, and play that over on your non-Euclidean tintype.

THE STATEMENT OF RANDOLPH CARTER

[LATE DECEMBER 1919]

This is just a shaggy-dog story, albeit a better one than "The Unnamable." Like "Dagon," it was based on one of Lovecraft's dreams, with him in the 'Randolph Carter' part and Samuel Loveman as 'Harley Warren.' Weirdly enough, Lovecraft and C.M. Eddy almost recapitulated this story in 1923, going in search of "Dark Swamp" near Chepachet, Rhode Island, but they couldn't find it. Given the amount of *Blair Witch*-esque wandering around in the woods that HPL did with his friends and alone, it's odd that he seldom uses that outdoorsy method of introducing the horror.

The big question, of course, is what *English-speaking* monsters could possibly have unnerved a fellow like Harley Warren? (Any number of things could have overpowered and eaten him, of course.) My current favorite notion is that the horde/swarm (whatever it is) attacks along, and consumes, the language center of its victim on a psychic level—becoming quite literally indescribable. (Kind of a cognitive-linguistic Gorgon or basilisk.) The act of perceiving, and attempting to make linguistic sense of, the creature(s) is thus a self-destroying act. (Again, like spearing a basilisk—its poison runs along the tool you use to apprehend it, and kills you.) By eating/absorbing Warren, it/they ate/absorbed *his* language center and could thus speak English to Carter.

Or, sure, they might have been ghouls.

THE TERRIBLE OLD MAN

[JANUARY 28, 1920]

Not actually a bad story, in an EC Comics kind of way, but far, far from Lovecraft's best. I don't find myself particularly annoyed by the arch diction (which Joshi, I think, is correct to derive from Dunsany's tales), and at least Lovecraft doesn't drag it out endlessly (a la "The Outsider") in an attempt to prolong the journey to the punch line.

****

And I really do like the Terrible Old Man, his necromantic bottles (which I've ripped off for a number of roleplaying game sessions since), and especially his front yard:

> *Among the gnarled trees in the front yard of his aged and neglected place he maintains a strange collection of large stones, oddly grouped and painted so that they resemble the idols in some obscure Eastern temple. This collection frightens away most of the small boys...*

This sentence-plus is nigh-perfectly done, although one might cavil at Lovecraft using "strange" and "oddly" to force the reader's conclusion.

****

Honesty compels us to admit that this is a Lovecraft story (although almost the only one) in which he gives ugly narrative (as opposed to descriptive) vent to his racism. Ethnic minorities (Ricci, Czanek, and Silva, as Joshi points out, represent Italians, Poles, and Portuguese, the three main non-Anglo immigrant groups in Providence in 1920) die horribly at the hands of Outside forces, directed by an old Anglo-Saxon New Englander. Worse yet, their deaths are obviously played for comic effect. Lovecraft dilutes some of the nasty taste by conflating Anglo-Saxon New England longevity with degeneration and horror (which he repeats in, for example, "Picture in the House," "He," *Charles Dexter Ward*, and even "Dunwich Horror"—all of which have Anglo-Saxon victims), but not all of it.

THE TREE

[SPRING? 1920]

Grecian argle-bargle from HPL, obviously modelled on Hawthorne's *Twice-Told Tales*, and just as obviously a mistaken choice by Lovecraft. I'm not sure why Lovecraft's historical fiction skills don't shine here, when his work in, say, *Charles Dexter Ward* demonstrates how good his historical sense was. Maybe it's just the seven years' difference in the writing dates. Maybe it's just that nothing much happens in the story at all, or that Lovecraft the writer was stultified by his own historical knowledge. For whatever reason, comparing "The Tree" to Robert E. Howard's historical fiction (written with a far more slapdash approach) is kind of depressing.

****

Far more interestingly, George Wetzel takes "The Tree" as an example of the unsung influence of the Greek myths on the Cthulhu Mythos, along with other early efforts such as "Hypnos," "The Moon-Bog," "The Crawling Chaos," "The Green Meadow," and the word '*Necronomicon*,' which is, at the very least, a Greek-ism of arcane antecedents if debatable quality. Wetzel has ahold of something there, specifically when he cites the rarely seen 1920 Lovecraft collaboration "Poetry and the Gods," from which I quote thusly:

> *In thy yearning hast thou divined what no mortal, saving only a few whom the world rejects, remembereth: that the Gods were never dead, but only sleeping the sleep and dreaming the dreams of Gods in lotos-filled Hesperian gardens beyond the golden sunset. And now draweth nigh the time of their awakening, when coldness and ugliness shall perish, and Zeus sit once more*

> on Olympus. Already the sea about Paphos trembleth into a foam which only ancient skies have looked on before, and at night on Helicon the shepherds hear strange murmurings and half-remembered notes. Woods and fields are tremulous at twilight with the shimmering of white saltant forms, and immemorial Ocean yields up curious sights beneath thin moons. The Gods are patient, and have slept long, but neither man nor giant shall defy the Gods forever. In Tartarus the Titans writhe and beneath the fiery Aetna groan the children of Uranus and Gaea. The day now dawns when man must answer for centuries of denial, but in sleeping the Gods have grown kind and will not hurl him to the gulf made for deniers of Gods. Instead will their vengeance smite the darkness, fallacy and ugliness which have turned the mind of man; and under the sway of bearded Saturnus shall mortals, once more sacrificing unto him, dwell in beauty and delight. This night shalt thou know the favour of the Gods, and behold on Parnassus those dreams which the Gods have through ages sent to earth to show that they are not dead. For poets are the dreams of Gods, and in each and every age someone hath sung unknowingly the message and the promise from the lotos gardens beyond the sunset.

Wetzel likewise suggests that Lovecraft the Epicurean modelled his Cthulhoid gods on Epicurus' deities, who remain blissfully unconcerned with—or even unconscious of—human affairs. (This, I think, would be the middle position between the generally upbeat apocalypse of "Poetry and the Gods" and the more familiar degeneracy-and-devastation eschaton of "Nyarlathotep," written about the same time.) Wetzel draws a number of specific parallels between Lovecraft's horror and fantasy worlds and the Greek myths, and I think in general he's correct to do so, if only because a) we know, from his own testimony, that HPL modelled his mythos on historical myth patterns, and b) almost the only historical myth pattern that Lovecraft understood in any sophistication was the Greek.

****

Myself, I've found reading Greek myths, and reading about Greek myths, to be particularly useful in constructing horror mythologies and secret histories, including and especially Lovecraftian ones. Although Robert Graves is a howling crazy person whose footnotes should not be trusted one iota, his anthology *The Greek Myths* will rapidly undo a great deal of the false certainty one gets from one's childhood reading of Hamilton, Bulfinch, D'Aulaire, et al. (I also recommend hitting the very fine Theoi.com website for a first cut at comparative Greek mythology.) The Greek mythic tradition extends over at least 900 years (and at least four geographically and culturally separate matrices: Ionia, Classical Greece, Hellenistic Egypt, and Rome) in written works alone, and as a body of worship it goes back another thousand years or so. The earliest work of Greek mythology, Hesiod's *Theogony*, is an attempt to rationalize and unify a hugely disparate body of pre-existing myths. (Hesiod was the Lin Carter, if you will, of the Greek mythos.) There is a palpable change (or rather, many palpable changes) since Hesiod in the whole tenor and character of written Greek myth, as well as in the patterns of worship and lived experience of Greek pagan religion.

Jane Ellen Harrison and F.M. Cornford and their ilk likewise went far too far, especially in imagining that they could suss out the "primitive" versions of the myths, but reading them is likewise a corrective to collapsing Hesiod and Ovid into one story, as well as a great way to creep yourself the hell out. I recommend E.R. Dodds' *The Greeks and the Irrational* as another study in that corrective tradition, and usefully, one that doesn't happen to be full of Frazerian bilge.

FACTS CONCERNING THE LATE ARTHUR JERMYN AND HIS FAMILY

[EARLY 1920?]

This will do as well as anywhere as a place to remind a 21st century readership that Lovecraft's racism is not somehow "separate" from his other thought, for all that it seldom takes the front row in his fictional themes. Lovecraft described himself as a blend of three streams of thought: antiquarianism, scientism, and the weird. His racism fully partakes of the first two. He clearly believed that the Anglo-Saxon culture of roughly the 18th-century "Augustan Era" was the high point of human aesthetic achievement, and strongly self-identified with it. He was a "cultural" racist, who believed that cultural admixture (and even assimilation) of foreigners, and especially Jews, was polluting what remained of that culture in New England, and in Anglo-Saxondom generally.

At the same time, his racism was thoroughly scientific. Lovecraft was an eager devotee of Ernst Haeckel, one of the leading lights of scientific racism. It's important to remember that in the 1920s biological racism was as much a scientific consensus as mitochondrial DNA counts are in our day. Lovecraft was not a crank, at least not as far as his science went. Indeed, his one "crank" belief, in Wegener's continental drift hypothesis, turned out to be correct. His cultural biases and his scientific knowledge didn't contradict each other, but instead reinforced each other, so he never had to pick one over the other.

Which leaves the weird—and the fraught (and oft-plumbed) question: Just how much of Lovecraft's sense of the weird and uncanny is, to say the least, racially charged? We're not going to be able to answer that question here, not more specifically than "some of it."

****

With all that under our belt: Okay, so Lovecraft was a racist. (And very much an anti-Semite, although to the atheist HPL, it was pretty much the same thing.) No question. He was probably more racist even than the average Yankee of his generation, and if not, he was certainly far more articulate in his racism. If you find that an insuperable problem—well, good luck reading Lovecraft. (Or pretty much anything else written between, say, 1700 and 1950.) That said, although "Arthur Jermyn" has some typically repellent Lovecraftian grace notes ("a loathsome black woman from Guinea") it's not actually about race per se.[7]

It's the first example, rather, of Lovecraft's constant theme of miscegenation. Miscegenation is a big, honking part of the Gothic tradition from which

HPL sprang. We have a hard time reading the Gothics this way, because (for the most part) we no longer instinctively recoil from Southern European Catholics in the way that English (and German) women of the 18th-19th centuries did (or at least thought they were supposed to). But much of the frisson of *Wuthering Heights*, for example, comes from Heathcliff's "gipsy" blood mingling with Catherine's "fair" self. If you can't (or won't) read it that way, you're missing out on some of its power—unless you consciously inflate Heathcliff's demonic monstrosity over and above his ethnicity. So it is with Lovecraft, who clearly consciously makes the same decision about his stories, to subsume any racial questions in the larger issues of monstrosity.

Thus, Lovecraft almost invariably codes miscegenation as intermixing between human and alien blood, rather than simple race-mixing, which becomes a signifier (albeit a racist signifier, obviously) of a deeper taint (often demon-worship) somewhere else. (Race-mixing can also become, as in "Arthur Jermyn" or "The Shadow Over Innsmouth," a red herring for the monstrous truth.) Now, obviously it's quite defensible to read Lovecraft's concern with miscegenation as tied in to his racism, and in the case of "Arthur Jermyn" specifically, coding apes as blacks, and vice versa, has a long and inglorious history before and after HPL. But that said, for all his whimpering about "mongrels," for HPL— as an artist, anyway— miscegenation is bigger than race.

Thus, a key element of "Arthur Jermyn" is the way that it implicates everyone, Lovecraft very much included ("If we knew what we are, we should do as Arthur Jermyn did...") in the taint of ape blood. (Joshi points out the coincidences between the Jermyn and Lovecraft lineages in his Penguin notes.) It may seem odd—heck, it *is* odd—that an atheist mechanist like HPL believed he could wring horror out of, essentially, an excit-

---

7. There's also a nasty little grace note toward the end, one which for whatever reason struck me as particularly foul. Jermyn makes a deal with a Belgian agent to acquire the ape-goddess from "the once mighty N'bangus...now the submissive servants of King Albert's government." The Belgian believes that the N'bangus "with but little persuasion could be induced to part with the gruesome deity..." Given the charnel nature of the Belgian Congo, reading Jermyn's willingness to traffic in genocide-enforced theft of sacred objects...well, eeeww. Though one can't mention the Congo and Lovecraft without adding a recommendation for David Drake's hammer-blow of a story, "Than Curse the Darkness."

able travesty of Darwin, but there you have it. In general, HPL's miscegenation-horror (unlike, say, Poe's) isn't the fear of the Other per se, or even of the Other threatening to violate our blood, but the fear that the Other is already inside us. (Having a father who dies a syphilitic madman will do that to you, I imagine.) This recurs not just in "The Outsider" but in HPL's unquestioned masterpieces: "The Shadow Over Innsmouth," *Charles Dexter Ward*, *At the Mountains of Madness*, and "The Shadow Out of Time" especially. The theme is a constant, and a different thing entirely from the purse-lipped descriptions of "polyglot swarming" neighborhoods we associate with HPL's race discourse. It almost seems as if Lovecraft talks himself into believing his code entirely—by his last story, "The Haunter of the Dark," the evil cult is held at bay by the kinds of people (southern Italians) he used to regard as symptomatic of corruption.

****

In our Oh So Enlightened Times, of course, we merely exoticize the Other instead of both demonizing it and exoticizing it, so I'll close with the notion that the gorilla-charming (and gorilla-fighting) circus baronet Sir Alfred Jermyn would make a fine member of the *League of Eldritch Gentlemen*.

THE CATS OF ULTHAR

[JUNE 15, 1920]

Another great story. Only its lightness of tone, in my opinion, keeps it from the utter perfection of "Sarnath," but this could be a sheerly personal judgement. I like my Lovecraft (and my horror) heavy, and lightness isn't Lovecraft's natural metier, although you certainly couldn't determine that from this story alone. No doubt his great, great love for *Felis d.* helped impel HPL to a deftness and playfulness of tone in this story that he seems unable to quite reach before or after.

****

When re-reading it in the Penguin edition for this entry, I noted Joshi's note no. 6, saying that young Menes' name is "probably derived from Dunsany's play *King Argimenes*." Perhaps I'm crazy, here, but doesn't it make far more sense that young Menes is derived from, indeed is supposed to be, Menes the (historical) first Pharaoh of the Two Lands of Egypt? Note the Egyptian motifs on his cart and amongst his entourage, and that Menes' people are "dark" compared to the Ultharians. (This, by the way, would be a reverse of "Terrible Old Man"—dark people use the Outside to punish lighter-skinned evildoers.)

If Menes is the future Pharaoh Menes, that means:

a) Ulthar is a historical city, and the story takes place around 3100 B.C., when Menes would have been a young boy, or:

b) Menes and the priest-magicians who would eventually found Memphis and unite Egypt spent some time in the Otherworld/Dreamlands/ distant past/Faërie, where they had adventures and gained knowledge necessary to unite Egypt, or:

c) The Pharaoh Menes is a small, wonder-working boy in the Dreamlands, much as Kuranes is a mundane writer in the waking world and a mighty pharaoh in Dreaming—which he might continue to inhabit in that form after his death, as does King Kuranes.

The preponderance of evidence would tend toward b), as the general tenor of Ulthar seems more cod-medieval than pre-Bronze Age, since there are inns and blacksmiths in Ulthar. Also, since Menes' folk come "from the South," that would imply that Ulthar is somewhere on the upper Nile Valley (later tales state that Ulthar is on the River Skai) if it's a historical location, and it's unlikely that a town in Nubia or Abyssinia would consider Egyptians "dark." Of course, Lovecraft could be gaming the situation; reversing the sojourn of Israel (with Menes as a kind of parallel to Joseph) by inventing a sojourn of proto-Egypt in the north. Or Ulthar could be a city north of the Sudan, in the future Egypt, settled by the Berbers or some "lost white race" of the primordial Saharan grassland.

The story, meanwhile, presents Menes' folk as Romany, or Gypsies, as much as anything else: their fortunetelling habits, itinerant lifestyle, decorated carts, and ethnic markers indicate as much. At the time, the Romany claimed to be exiles from Egypt (hence the name 'Gypsy'), and 19th century occultists decided that 'Gypsy fortunetelling' was actually lost (and debased) Egyptian wisdom. It would be a typically arch Lovecraftian touch to imply that 'Egyptian wisdom' began as Gypsy fortunetelling, cloud-magic, and cat-cursing, and that the whole thing turned in cycles.

Or, of course, c) might be the correct answer, and Menes, like Randolph Carter, was self-created by his dreams of boyhood. Pharaoh dreaming of a boy whose wonders would unite Egypt and make him Pharaoh. Or perhaps, pace "Polaris," Ulthar is the real city, and Egypt is just the cloud-mirage.

****

Like "The Terrible Old Man," "The Doom That Came to Sarnath," and "The Tree," this story has a pretty straightforward "punishment of the sinner" message that many critics find uncongenial. Lovecraft, too, seems to have found it so: "In the Vault," a 1925 story, is the last one in this direct mode. Most sufferers in Lovecraft after 1925 (as well as a goodly number before that date, of course) commit only the sin of Faust, that of seeking knowledge beyond their power, and such Faustian dreams often have a sort of doomed nobility to them (*Charles Dexter Ward*, *At the Mountains of Madness*). We can, however, read "The Dunwich Horror" (1928) as a kind of last gasp of the "sinner narrative," a sort of Rosetta stone linking it to the more orthodox Lovecraftian message of inevitable cosmic doom.

The Temple

[Summer/fall 1920?]

A fine little tale, and another example of the Lovecraftian "Otherworld/Underworld" motif. This motif recurs from "Dagon" through (among others) "White Ship," "Celephaïs," "Festival" and *Dream-Quest* through the Johansen narrative in "The Call of Cthulhu" and "The Shadow Over Innsmouth". In it, a dreaming, hallucinating, mad, or otherwise unreliable narrator travels across (or, often, explicitly under) the ocean to the Other/Underworld, usually through a stretch of phosphorescence or other witchlight, usually with fatal or near-fatal consequences.

Likewise, the cursed figurine is another bead on the string of Lovecraft's "cursed sculpture" topoi: the idols of Bokrug and Cthulhu from "Sarnath" and "Call," the amulet in "The Hound," the tiara in "Innsmouth," and finally the Shining Trapezohedron that summons "The Haunter of the Dark." All open the holder or viewer to the Outside, usually with unfortunate consequences. (The bust in "Hypnos" is kind of the reverse—like the wax mask in "Whisperer" it serves to confirm an encounter as definitively one with the Outside.) The positive version, the "magic artifact," happens almost never in Lovecraft, outside the titular "Silver Key," although that may be prefigured by the key in "The Tomb."

The "cursed artifact" moves from sculpture through bas-relief (in "Nameless City" and *At the Mountains of Madness*), two-dimensional image (the titular "Picture in the House," both paintings and photograph in "Pickman's Model," the portrait in *Charles Dexter Ward*), through lines of text (the *Necronomicon*, *Pnakotic Manuscripts*, et al. down to the drifts of tomes in "Haunter"), to a mere geometrical figure ("Dreams in the Witch House"). Or the sculpture can move outward, to architecture that opens the way Outside, as do Exham Priory in "Rats in the Walls" and the titular structures in "The Shunned House" and "The Strange High House in the

Mist," as well as the various necropoleis from the Nameless City to R'lyeh to Kadath to Pnakotus. The third direction—from art to science—leads our "cursed artifact" toward, say, the core-sampling drills in *At the Mountains of Madness* or better still, the resonator in "From Beyond," which literally opens the way to the Outside for its unfortunate possessor.

An early Lovecraftian attempt at character study, too; marred for some by excessive jingoism, but you can't say that Lieutenant-Commander Karl Heinrich's voice doesn't stand out amid Lovecraft's other narrators.

But the real question is this—this story was written in 1920. Is it the first literary "haunted submarine" tale? If not, it's darned close to it. People often think of Lovecraft as a quaint, period-piece, pulp writer, but at the time he was writing, he was writing some cutting-edge techno-horror.

CELEPHAÏS

[EARLY NOVEMBER 1920]

I confess that I find most of HPL's 'Dunsanian' works second-rate, except for "The Cats of Ulthar" and "The Doom That Came to Sarnath," which latter is almost perfect pastiche.

But in service to our project, I re-read "Celephaïs" and found that it makes a whole lot more sense, or is at least a whole lot more fun, if you treat Ooth-Nargai, et al., as Faërie. Then, it's the fairly creepy (not least because quasi-sympathetic) story of a man seduced by the Other Side, not a mawkish exercise in artistic self-pity and whining. Indeed, read thusly, it merits comparison with Machen's "The White People," which is not something I would have thought remotely plausible before now. Of course, even read as a faerie story, "Celephaïs" isn't nearly as strong as "The White People." But it can be defensibly considered to be playing in the same ballpark, or at least in the same league.

That said, I think HPL intended it to be artistic criticism as much as anything, and it fails at that resoundingly, not least because the story doesn't actually obey its own dictates, striving far too clumsily for effect rather than acheiving effortless transmission of antique beauty. But again, it was a very early, very amateurish effort.

NYARLATHOTEP

[NOVEMBER 1920]

Although we get bits of it in "Dagon":

I dream of a day when they may rise above the billows to drag down in their reeking talons the remnants of puny, war-exhausted mankind—of a day when the land shall sink, and the dark ocean floor shall ascend amidst universal pandemonium.

and a hint in "Arthur Jermyn":

Science, already oppressive with its shocking revelations, will perhaps be the ultimate exterminator of our human species...for its reserve of unguessed horrors could never be borne by mortal brains if loosed upon the world.

it's in "Nyarlathotep" that we get Lovecraft's full-blown Apocalypse. Like "Dagon," "Statement of Randolph Carter," and "Celephaïs" written from a dream, this prose-poem doesn't even pretend to have a plot. It's all incident. The parallels to the Book of Revelation are obvious—we have the turmoil of war and weather, and a harbinger figure emerges (out of Egypt, not Babylon—but then Christ came "out of Egypt" at least once) for his Second Coming, spreading an almost literally Antichrist-like gospel of technology and nightmare. He "opens the seals" and shows a vision of the end of the world, which then happens, leaving the New Heaven and Earth unified in Him. It's really, really good, and repays re-reading both for under-emphasized tropes in Lovecraft (as in "He" and "Shadow Out of Time," the Yellow Peril conquers the world in the future) and for language and theme. Only Castro's ranting apocalypse from "Call of Cthulhu" is its equal, and it's distanced by being placed in another voice.

****

I will lose my eliptonist's license if I don't note that pulp scholar Will Murray has theorized that Lovecraft based this story on the "electrical showman" tours conducted by Nikola Tesla around the turn of the century. Speaking in my skeptic's voice, I don't believe it—there's no evidence—but I'd accept the notion that Tesla put some of the flavor into the atmosphere that Lovecraft drew on for Nyarlathotep's atmospherics: "Then the sparks played amazingly around the head of the spectators" certainly sounds Tesla-ish, but the rest is just wishful thinking of the sort I heartily endorse.

FROM BEYOND

[NOVEMBER 16, 1920]

"From Beyond" is evidence that I will overlook the worst excesses (and this story, in Darrell Schweitzer's apt description, gibbers from start to finish) of Lovecraft's early Poe-influenced style if he's using it in the service of an actual Lovecraftian concept.

Here, Lovecraft revisits "Fall of the House of Usher," (as he will again, far more ably, in "Rats in the Walls") with a hyper-sensitive madman and his mostly anonymous guest, who exists almost solely to hear the exposition unfold and to plausibly describe the madman's destruction. But where we see further (and more horribly) into Usher in Poe's tale, in this one we see further (and more horribly) into the truth of the Universe.

I consider "From Beyond" to be an almost critical story for understanding the Cthulhu Mythos, despite its narrative flatness and the absence of any of the great names. Rather, its very simplicity of construction and paucity of specific myth-cycle linkage allows it to serve as a skeleton key to the more sophisticated later stories. This story is entirely a disquisition on the nature of the Outside.

We learn that the Outside is:

- Much vaster than the perceptible cosmos, and that our dimensionality (including time) is purely local.
- Entirely interpenetrative of our universe; as Uncle Chu would say, "The Outside is here, Mister Burton."
- Largely (even entirely) independent of our concerns.
- Horribly dangerous, both physically and mentally, to those who encounter it, even fleetingly.
- Inhabited by entities, both sentient and non-, as well as by intelligences that transcend sapience.
- Possessed of its own hierarchies, ecologies, and struggles.
- Accessible by human (and logically by in- or pre-human) technology.
- When so accessed, capable of being harnessed or of expanding human abilities in ways strongly resembling legendary magic.

This metaphysics becomes common to the rest of Lovecraft's oeuvre. With this metaphysics established, Lovecraft spends the rest of his career learning the exact ratio of Outsideness to put in a story, and the need for rigorous verisimilitude, even calm, in the "material components" of a tale. His best stories, are those that skirt the line between reality and Outsideness; what the radical critic Paul Buhle has so interestingly phrased thusly:

> *Lovecraft's true strength, then, lay in his ability to give the modern sense of indeterminacy a weird and poetic interpretation. What man feared was not correctly speaking the 'Unknown'…[but]…being on the verge of rediscovering something terrible and arcane…the more threatening because in another sense it was known already….*

I like Buhle's nod to Heisenberg in this quote, and the way it grounds Lovecraftian cosmicism not just in quantum physics (which, like the Tillinghast resonator, demonstrates just how meager our world of Newtonian experience and inference really is) but also Theosophy; the sense of knowledge that predates, but somehow informs, humanity. The Theosophical component is mostly absent from "From Beyond," but the Heisenbergian component of the Mythos is never clearer.

THE PICTURE IN THE HOUSE

[DECEMBER 12, 1920]

Lovecraft wrote some great first lines in his day, but there's only one or two that can stand up there with "Seekers after horror haunt strange, far places." The trouble is that people seem to miss his further point, in the delight of the phrase—that your own backyard is scarier still, if you stop to look. This was one of Lovecraft's unsung contributions to horror; bringing it home rather than setting it in "Italy" or "Geneva" or "Transylvania" or some nebulous no-place like Poe did. (Poe, after all, boasted: "Horror is not of Germany, but of the soul." Yes, *but*.) True, Machen had the same instinct on occasion, and Stoker was clever enough to briefly bring a foreign vampire into the beating heart of Victorian London, but Lovecraft did it more intensely than either. And yes, HPL did his share of globetrotting writing. But all that said, this seeking after horror at home is one of Lovecraft's sterling "Copernican Revolutions" of weird fiction; no less influential for all the occasional Aristarchuses and Nicolases of Cusa before him. There'd be no Stephen King Maine without Lovecraft's New England; it's the richness of reference to something you know intimately that separates the real from the phony.

We'll leave our introduction of the "familiar setting" revolution with this very striking HPL quote, from a November 1930 letter to Clark Ashton Smith:

> *I want to know what stretches Outside, & to be able to visit all the gulfs & dimensions beyond Space & Time. I want, too, to juggle the calendar at will; bringing things from the immemorial past down to the present, & making long journeys into the forgotten years. But I want the familiar Old Providence of my childhood as a perpetual base for these necromancies & excursions—& in a good part of these necromancies & excursions I want certain transmuted features of Old Providence to form parts of the alien voids I visit or conjure up. I am as geographic-minded as a cat—places are everything to me.*

Keep that quote in mind, especially once we get to Antarctica.

****

This, to make a very unfair comparison, is partially why I'm less than impressed with the adequate horror-pulp Harry Dresden novels by Jim Butcher. They're supposedly set in Chicago, but for all the Chicago-ness they exhibit, they might as well be set in Arkham, or Metropolis. Or Toronto, which is apparently where they're filming the TV show.

****

It's fun to peel the layers back on the titular picture, which is of a cannibal feast of "the Anziques." (Again, HPL avoids centering on race, noting instead that the "Anziques" are depicted "with Caucasian features.") Just now, I told you about the picture, as written by Lovecraft, as relayed by the narrator, as described by the Old Man, as illustrated by "the brothers De Bry," from text printed in a Latin edition, of a book originally written in Italian, by an author telling another traveler's story. That's eight levels between you and the cannibal feast. (And since HPL never actually saw a copy of *Regnum Congo*, but depended on descriptions and some reproductions in book by T.H. Huxley, that's either one or two more levels in there somewhere.) This is a raw version of the interleaved, almost archaeological narrative that HPL will come to master fully in "The Call of Cthulhu."

****

One more great phrase from the story, less well-known than the opener: "hungry fer victuals I couldn't raise nor buy..." *Brrrrr.*

THE NAMELESS CITY

[MID- TO LATE JANUARY 1921]

This is a fairly annoying story, in that it contains far too many good, powerful ideas than should be allowed in a story this badly written. One would like to just ignore it and move on, but one really can't.

****

I'll just note, for those joining us late, that the Nameless City is *not* Irem of the Pillars. The legend of Irem served as Lovecraft's model, but here again as with Ib/Sarnath we see our city-cycle unfold, this time as a sort of photo-negative. The Nameless City spawns (?) the human imitation city Irem; Irem appears as the Nameless City dries out; the debased remnants of the Nameless City tear "a pioneer of ancient Irem" to pieces; the Nameless City's inhabitants enter the hollow earth. In the Arabic legend, the same pattern: Irem is riding for a fall as Mecca rises; the debased Iremites drive off Hud (the lone "pioneer" from Mecca); Irem sinks into the sands.

****

Joshi is correct to notice that Lovecraft does the "history of the aliens by convenient bas-relief" better in *At the Mountains of Madness*, although even there it's just never very convincing. The psychic visions of Robert Blake in "Haunter of the Dark" are at least plausible.

****

It is interesting to note that this, too, like "Dagon" and "The Temple" and "Festival" and "Celephaïs" and *Dream-Quest* and "Shadow Over Innsmouth," is one of the "Oceanic Underworld/Otherworld" motif stories. The reptiles are aquatic (crocodile-seal blend), the Nameless City was a seaport, the Moore poem quoted (to better effect than Alhazred, in fact) mentions the "Sea of Death," and the narrator fights "swirling currents" and a "torrent." Lovecraft repeatedly plays with words like "abyss" and "gulf," which can apply to caverns and ocean deeps alike. The inner world of the reptiles ("a sea of sunlit mist") even resembles both the "Dreamlands" and Y'ha-Nthlei: "glorious cities and ethereal hills and valleys." Finally, Lovecraft took partial inspiration for this tale from a dream in which the protagonist in a "subterranean chamber—seeks to force door of bronze—overwhelmed by influx of waters." Dreamland, Underworld, Ocean, Otherworld.

****

But how on earth does someone who can compose the wonderful simile of the ruins "protruding uncannily above the sands as parts of a corpse may protrude from an ill-made grave" manage to let themselves write, not a page later, that the "brooding ruins…swelled beneath the sand like an ogre under a coverlet." It's like a Randall Garrett Lovecraft parody in its pluperfect wrongness. And it ain't gonna get any better for the next five stories, sadly.

THE QUEST OF IRANON

[FEBRUARY 1921]

One would be tempted to call this story Lovecraft's riff on Robert W. Chambers' "Repairer of Reputations," which also concerns the fall of someone with delusions of royalty, except that HPL didn't read that story until 1927. As it is, it's more likely Lovecraft's riff on Dunsany's "Carcassonne," and the interesting thing is that in 1921 Lovecraft's prose is very much improved by his effort to pastiche Dunsany. Where faux-Poe unleashes all of Lovecraft's bad purpuric habits without adding any of Poe's genius for psychology, faux-Dunsany restrains Lovecraft, forcing him to hit a rhythm, while adding HPL's superior instinct for plot to mitigate Dunsany's occasional Irish tendency to aimless (though beautiful) blather.

****

The similarity between the fate of Iranon and the fate of returnees from the Otherworld (I'm thinking specifically of Herla's men, but there are others) is another chalk-mark for our habit of reading the so-called "Dreamland" stories as "Faërie" stories instead. We might thus also consider Iranon an early example of what Wetzel would have called the "changeling motif" in Lovecraft, which he develops more powerfully with the ghouls and Deep Ones.

****

And let's note, too, that like Leng and Kadath, Sarnath and Lomar (both of which feature in this tale) also show up in Lovecraft's "real world"—the boundary between "Dreamland" stories and "Mythos" stories is so thin as to be risible. As thin, indeed, as one suspects Lovecraft considers the boundaries between the mundane world and any of his higher dimensions (the ultraviolet, hyperspace, the Dreamlands, the past of "He" and "The Tomb," or the chaos outside Erich Zann's window), or the boundary between life and death in "Cool Air" and "Herbert West" and "Pickman's Model." Thin-ness of boundaries, the lack of walls between the Mad and the True or the Sacred and the Profane (or, reductively, the Anglo-Saxon and the Foreign), seems to be a huge meta-concern spanning all of Lovecraft's work.

The Moon-Bog

[Early March 1921]

The saving grace of "The Moon-Bog" is that Lovecraft doesn't appear to have cared enough about it to over-write, or at least he doesn't fill every scintilla of narrative space with his Poe-esque spasms. On the other hand, aside from one or two concepts that will pay off big in later works—such as the notion of archaeology as the Gothic sin of 'awakening the past'— and another intriguing example of lunar trouble (along with "Sarnath"), this story, by its very pro forma nature, is almost worse than something like "The Outsider."

****

Again, though, I like the use of Greek myth as Elder Horror.

****

For racism-watchers, it's interesting to note that despite the anti-Irish sentiments he sometimes expressed in HPL's letters ("try and reason with an Irishman!"), the simple Irish workmen in this story are far more notable for their class than their ethnicity. They're not even the colorful, childlike Irish country folk you meet in, say, Ray Bradbury's Irish tales, but rather generic peasants, who drop exposition in their "wild legendry," bustle about as servants, and then get kidnapped by the Fair Folk, er, naiads. The story could just as easily have been set in England (as its great descendant "The Rats in the Walls" was) or Pomerania or Spain; a remarkable deafness to setting from HPL, although the bog itself is a familiar New England swamp. For "The Moon-Bog," HPL chose the setting because the piece was meant for a St. Patrick's Day meeting of his amateur fiction group; Dunsany aside, Lovecraft doesn't seem to have felt Ireland or the Irish to be much of an inspiration, for good or ill. Indeed, the only other

Irishmen named as such in all of Lovecraft's fiction are Detective Malone the "Dublin College man" from "Horror at Red Hook," and the "great wholesome" policeman in "Haunter of the Dark." While casting the Irish as good cops over their heads won't win Lovecraft any awards for creative thinking, it's not nearly as bad as it could have been.

In Lovecraft's correspondence with Robert E. Howard, who claimed to be of "Celtic stock," they seem to have agreed that the Celt provided a necessary leavening of poetry and magic to the hardy and stolid Anglo-Saxon, and that was about it. (Seriously, though, even in our enlightened era, who doesn't have a little bit of that antique ethnography still rattling around in their brain?) One suspects that between Dunsany, Maturin, Stoker, and LeFanu, Lovecraft may not have shared quite the disdain and contempt for the Irish that his self-image as an 18th-century Englishman would otherwise demand.

THE OUTSIDER

[SUMMER 1921]

Just to start off, I think that there's very little that can improve on Lovecraft's own self-criticism:

> *To my mind this tale—written a decade ago—is too glibly mechanical in its climactic effect, & almost comic in the bombastic pomposity of the language. As I re-read it, I can hardly understand how I could have let myself be tangled up in such baroque & windy rhetoric as recently as ten years ago. It represents my literal though unconscious imitation of Poe at its very height.*

I haven't got the vaguest idea why August Derleth made it the title tale of his first Lovecraft compendium, and I've got mostly condescending, insulting ideas why it seems to take such central place in Lovecraft criticism since. (Because it's a great, bloody obvious hook for various forms of cheap or downright meretricious psychoanalysis, is why, for starters.) I will allow that if you're interested in Lovecraft's stories as studies of the human condition, as opposed to dissections of the human position in the universe, "The Outsider" is probably your "From Beyond." I have a very hard time believing that someone who is both as tremendous a writer, and as manifestly mediocre at (because uninterested in) characterization, as Lovecraft was, can profitably be read that way, but you pays your money and so forth.

That said, lyrically, it's just bad Poe. Derleth wrote that if discovered in an attic with no author's name "The Outsider" would "pass for a lost tale of Poe," to which I would add that there would be little doubt why Poe left it unsigned and put it in an attic. It's not that the lugubrious, purple style of the thing is bad, in and of itself—Poe could, and did, churn out prose much like it, in really good stories. But in "The Outsider," it's just not in service to anything. Where Poe uses the warm fog of such language to create a psychological sensation linking the reader and narrator while exploring the narrator's inner life, Lovecraft's wordage is just larded on to extend the distance to the ending (which he lifted from Hawthorne).

Lovecraft adds insult to injury by using an epigraph from Keats' "The Eve of St. Agnes," which is as full of sex and life and genuine mystery as "The Outsider" isn't.

Amazingly enough, George Wetzel manages to say something actually interesting about the piece on a mythical level, so I'll rip him off. He casts "The Outsider" as one chapter in Lovecraft's evolving ghoul-cycle, pointing out that the tale's combination of crypts, dreams, and a decayed corpse with fading (or ancient) human memory are all topoi of Lovecraft's ghouls. For Wetzel, the ghoul-cycle begins with the unnatural extension of life through cannibalism in "Picture in the House," continues with the twin themes of self-discovery and buried ancestral horror in "The Outsider" and "The Rats in the Walls," and emerges triumphantly in "Pickman's Model" and *Dream-Quest*, where the full ouroborous pattern of the ghouls is revealed. Although it's dressing the corpse in borrowed cerements, I have to say this is almost a convincing reason to re-read "The Outsider."

THE OTHER GODS

[AUGUST 14, 1921]

By comparison, here is an example of a failed Dunsany pastiche. Lovecraft attempts Dunsany's lightly terrifying (or terrifyingly light) parable mode (as shown to best effect in *Gods of Pegana* and *Time and the Gods*) and, as one might expect, comes crashing to earth like Atal the priest. "Ulthar" notwithstanding, delicate arabesque was not Lovecraft's metier, especially not in 1921, and double-especially not when he attempted to combine it with cosmic sublimity. Where Dunsany was a musical fabulist, all silver and moonbeams, Lovecraft was a Gothic architect; he worked in stone and leaded glass, and it is a tribute to HPL's powers in his own media that his later works fling up such vertiginous traceries of language and concept (eventually surpassing Dunsany).

****

I forget which writer it was (Faulkner? O. Henry?) who gave something like this advice to his colleagues: Cross out the first page of every story. Then keep crossing out paragraphs until you get to the actual beginning.

This isn't actually true with most Lovecraft. The prolonged serpentine advance from mundanity to Otherness is usually vitally necessary; Lovecraft's intricate structure requires such a survey for its foundations.

But this is not the case with a pure fable. Specifically, "The Other Gods" would be immensely better without its first five paragraphs. I'd also venture to say that it would improve mightily if it followed Lovecraft's standard terminal-climax structure and ended three paragraphs earlier. Re-read that middle section, beginning with "Hatheg-Kla is far in the stony desert..." and ending with "Merciful gods of earth, I am falling into the sky!" and see if I'm not right.

HERBERT WEST—REANIMATOR

[SEPTEMBER 1921-JUNE 1922]

Re-reading this piece, it's not nearly as terrible as I remember it being. Perhaps this is because I'm low-balling it, but I don't think so; it's a genuinely rollicking story, although not without stylistic discord. If it didn't have to keep summarizing itself (the editor was an idiot) it would be still better.

****

"Reanimator" is one of the earlier uses of (I would argue) a good fictional trait fairly specific to HPL—the exercise of Lovecraftian philosophy, by a Lovecraft character, ends in disaster. (Imagine an Ayn Rand novel in which the selfish, brilliant protagonist dies hated, miserable, impoverished, and alone. Or, to bring it down a notch, a Robert E. Howard story where the proud barbarian is tricked by the wily city folk and winds up exhibited in a zoo or pulling a manure cart for a plantation.) Herbert West, like Lovecraft, believes that life is purely chemical—and demonstrates that belief, and inevitably loses not only his life (in gruesome fashion) but earlier, his scientific mind as well (replacing it with "mere morbid and ghoulish curiosity"). In what we might call his "suicide-by-philosophy" trope, Lovecraft regularly kills his Mary Sues, often for the crime of *believing what Lovecraft believes*. Not always—Randolph Carter survives where Charles Dexter Ward doesn't (although Joshi argues fairly plausibly that both those novels are conscious epilogues to previous Lovecraftian aesthetics)—but more often than not.

****

Re-reading the story, I was struck again by the sheer awesomeness of Herbert West's tissue culture:

> ...*obtained from the nearly hatched eggs of an indescribable tropical reptile...It was better than human material for maintaining life in organless fragments, and that was now my friend's chief activity. In a dark corner of the laboratory, over a queer incubating burner, he kept a large covered vat full of this reptilian cell-matter; which multiplied and grew puffily and hideously.*

I swear, if I ever came up with something that neat, I'd take the rest of the week off.

THE MUSIC OF ERICH ZANN

[DECEMBER 1921]

> *Even when I break away, it is generally only through imitating something else! There are my "Poe" pieces & my "Dunsany" pieces—but alas—where are my Lovecraft pieces?*
>
> — H.P. LOVECRAFT, LETTER TO
> ELIZABETH TOLDRIDGE, MARCH 8 1929

In this oft-quoted passage (made popular by—sigh—August Derleth while taxonomizing HPL's fiction), Lovecraft is actually referring to his poetry. Even the harshly self-critical HPL admitted that, by 1929, "Only in some of my more realistic fictional prose do I shew any signs of developing, at this late date, a style of my own." In my estimation, "The Music of Erich Zann" (written in 1921) is the first, and among the finest, of his "Lovecraft pieces." Neither Poe nor Dunsany could have conceptualized it.

In it, Lovecraft calves away almost everything except the pure cosmic horror; there are no eldritch tomes, no mongrel swarms of dubious ethnicity, no invocations of Kjh'nrujd, the Masher of the Keyboard. There isn't even any exposition, and certainly no closure—Zann's narrative ("a full account in German of all the marvels and terrors which beset him") is literally blown away into the void. Joshi complains that the tale is *too* minimalist, which is a bit rich coming from him.

Likewise, the prose is carefully rationed, the adjectives used as buttresses, not as gargoyles. The leitmotif of silence and sound is perfectly maintained throughout, from the "silent and reticent" residents of the Rue d'Auseil through the "howling" music played by the mute violin-cellist to the absence of wind at the end. The story is almost elemental in structure, while still being entirely evocative and unsettling. Lovecraft even manages to limn Paris—if only the Paris of Hugo or Leroux—in a few architectural details, performing the difficult task of providing setting and anchor for a story that takes place almost entirely in two rooms of an anonymous boarding-house.

****

Note, by the way, how Lovecraft underlines the unnamability of the horror—it's literally never expressed in words. The German narrative disappears before it can be read, and the music defies words and description. But it occurs to me that, like Walter Gilman's hyperspatial insights, Zann's music—and the music that the Outside plays through his frozen corpse—could be expressed in mathematics.

Hypnos

[March? 1922]

Okay, "Hypnos" is just crazy-making. It's chock full of vitally interesting bits. First of all, there's the strong hint that the narrator's friend is the spirit of Edgar Allan Poe: immense brow, dark liquid eyes, black hair, dreamer, aged forty as Poe was when he died, references to "The Tell-Tale Heart" and "The Man in the Crowd" among other Poe tales, and the Poe-esque structure of the story itself. Plus, there's the "evil star" business again, more Greek myth, the possibilities of time-travel and destiny loops (done better, or at least more interestingly, than in "The Silver Key"), and the allusions to Einstein (complimentary) and Freud (dismissive). Even the setting—the London demimonde—is interesting in its oddly random way, and there's weird sexual-obsession vibes with the whole Muse angle which not even Lovecraft could have been unaware of.

Plus, the story gives another example of Lovecraftian supra-dimensional magic, blending "dream travel" a la Randolph Carter and hyperspatial exploration a la Walter Gilman. The narrator's description of their experiments sounds an awful lot like a path-working in the modern Western occult tradition—which is weird, because this is too early for HPL to have read anything by Crowley or the like. Lovecraft's exposure to the formal occult remained very, very sketchy for someone of his interests and profession, he being far more interested (justifiably so given his narrative priorities) in authentic ghost and witch lore. He eventually tracked down and read Waite's *Book of Ceremonial Magic*, but that was years after writing this story—as late as 1926 he was bemoaning his inability to find a copy.

But for all that, "Hypnos" just doesn't cohere. The bits fall all over the place, and the magic is just arbitrarily shoveled out. Part of this incoherence is intentional—it's another unreliable narrator story, of course, and better at it than "Dagon." Part of it is the occasional lurch into hysterical language in misbegotten imitation of Poe. (Yes, the narrator is a hysteric. But read this and, say, "The Black Cat" side by side, and see which one is clear when it needs to be and which one isn't.) But a big part of it is just that I don't think Lovecraft had it in him, in 1922, to do justice to the whole concept of human psychic exploration of the inhuman. (As contrasted with human physical, or even intellectual, exploration of the inhuman, a narrative that HPL clearly mastered: see *At the Mountains of Madness* for a seamless braiding of both.) And indeed, given that "The Dreams in the Witch House" doesn't quite fulfill its potential either, maybe he never did.

But man, a bad story has no business being this good. It's like biting into a Jack-in-the-Box burger and realizing that some fool has made it with what began as Kobe beef.

THE HOUND

[OCTOBER 1922]

A silly story about silly people. Perhaps only someone as sexless as Lovecraft could describe the self-proclaimed decadence of these two aesthetes so hilariously, although Wilde could possibly have taken a run at it, if he'd been in the mood for a little self-parody. (Joshi claims "The Hound" is self-parody, and it certainly has something of that Kim Newman mashup feel, between the shout-outs to Beckford, Doyle, Poe, Bierce, and Huysmans.) If one ever filmed it, it would almost have to be with two hyper-serious adolescents, to keep the feel correct. Down to the brand names and set design—the endless Lovecraftian "Gother than thou" catalogue never seems more endless than in these introductory paragraphs, which borrow cred from the Symbolists, the pre-Raphaelites, the Decadents, Baudelaire, Huysmans, and Goya, while one can only double up in helpless laughter at the notion of "nauseous musical instruments" for the production of "dissonances of exquisite morbidity and cacodaemoniacal ghastliness."

Plus, the only attempt ever put to paper to wring *italicized horror* from the words "in the Dutch language."

****

But I like "The Hound" far above its merits. Not only does it introduce the *Necronomicon*, and give that lovely shout-out to the "corpse-eating cult of inaccessible Leng, in Central Asia," when I first read it as a hyper-serious adolescent, it actually worked for me. The titular hound is also just a really cool monster, an astral projection (literally, "the ghastly soul-symbol") of the Dutch ghoul-lich who somehow learned the secrets of Leng way back in the 15th century. Indeed, the lich may have stolen the hound-amulet, and yet somehow escaped its judgement.

****

Judgement, need I remind you, that arrives "astride a Bacchanale of bats from night-black ruins of buried temples of Belial." Astride…a Bacchanale…of bats…*chittering in the Dutch language!*

THE LURKING FEAR

[MID- TO LATE NOVEMBER 1922]

There was thunder in the air on the night I went to the deserted mansion atop Tempest Mountain to find the lurking fear.
— H.P. LOVECRAFT, "THE LURKING FEAR"

Or in other, better-written, words, "It was a dark and stormy night."

This is Lovecraft's best terrible story. It is so artificial ("Thank God I did not then know what it was, else I should have died. But I was saved by the very thunder that had summoned it…"), and so overblown ("an earth verminous with millions of cannibal devils"), and so ludicrous ("Baleful primal trees…") that it slithers—through tiramisu-rich prose that might as well be heavy metal lyrics ("a wolf-fanged ghost that rode the midnight lightning")—all the way to the summit of high camp. Although Joshi is far too ready to play the "self-parody" card to justify Lovecraft's more godawful slop, it is impossible to believe, in this story at least, that HPL wasn't doing some portion of it on purpose, given the letter he wrote about this time on the pleasures of giving in to pure hackery.

****

History had led me to this archaic grave. History, indeed, was all I had after everything else ended in mocking Satanism.
— H.P. LOVECRAFT, "THE LURKING FEAR"

But even in the midst of such squamosity we see the outlines of a vast form rising. Just as "Reanimator" introduces Lovecraft's intriguing and eventually quite productive trope of the suicide-by-philosophy, "Lurking Fear" (written in the same slam-bang, damn-the-climax style, and for the same cheapskate client) introduces the suicide-by-history, the protagonist whose interest in uncovering the past leads to his doom. It's prefigured as suicide-by-archaeology in "Moon-Bog" and "Nameless City," of course, but this tale is the first explicit narrative engagement at length with the researcher-hero. It transposes the exposition as narration into exposition as narrative—rather than the author filling us in on the history of the Jermyn family, we have the protagonist read up on the Martenses, and we read over his shoulder, as it were. (Lovecraft's increasing skill in thus emotionally identifying us—the curious reader—with the protagonist doomed for his curiosity is perhaps under-emphasized in critical comment.) This trope flowers in almost all of Lovecraft's Great Works, directly in "Call of Cthulhu," *Charles Dexter Ward*, "Innsmouth," and "Haunter of the Dark" and at close approach (often, again, as archaeology) in *At the Mountains of Madness*, "Shadow Out of Time," "He," "Whisperer in Darkness" and various of the revisions such as "The Mound."

It approaches "Whisperer in Darkness" not merely in that element, and in a shared note of Fortean-cryptid ghost-hunting, but in the very un-Lovecraftian arena of character. Our unnamed narrator (whose "love of the grotesque and the terrible... has made [his] career a series of quests for strange horrors in literature and in life") is much like the folklorist Wilmarth, with perhaps Randolph Carter as a third dimension for what George Wetzel might well call the ur-Investigator, the detective in the great mystery novel—or mystery play—that Lovecraft was writing. Badly, at first.

The Rats in the Walls

[LATE AUGUST OR EARLY SEPTEMBER 1923]

With all due respect to his two perfect Dunsany pastiches ("The Cats of Ulthar" and "The Doom that Came to Sarnath") and to the under-rated "The Music of Erich Zann," "The Rats in the Walls" is Lovecraft's first fully-throated horror masterpiece. If Lovecraft had suddenly chucked it all away in March 1924, or gone on to write nothing but architectural travelogues, this story would still be remembered and anthologized.

With stories this good, I don't propose to spend quite as much effort dragging out their structure and such, or summarizing previous criticism.[8] I can't help, however, joyously remarking on the deft way Lovecraft turns Poe's "House of Usher" inside out with this one. We get the same conceptual play on words, as Delapore descends simultaneously into the putrid bowels of his "house" (Exham Priory) and his "house" (the De la Poer lineage). Like Usher, Delapore's line is extinct—his son dies of his WWI injuries. We get the same excitation of the sense of hearing as the symptom, almost the literal entry-way, for the horror.[9] But unusually for Poe, "Usher" is not particularly (or at least not entirely) fixated on Usher's interior psychological life, whereas equally unusually for Lovecraft, "Rats" is very much concerned with the interior life of Delapore. In this story, Lovecraft

---

8. I would like to point out that again, Lovecraft removes, or denatures, race from his source material even as he emphasizes lineage and ethnicity. HPL borrowed the stress-atavism concept from a rather distasteful story by Irvin S. Cobb in which a Frenchman of mixed blood, run over by a train, cries out in an African dialect words used by his ancestor who had been gored by a rhinoceros. Sadly, of course, Lovecraft named Delapore's cat in the story after his own beloved cat Nigger-Man, and there are those "howling negroes" on the old family plantation (Carfax, a lovely *Dracula* tribute), so there you go with that. In other, happier racist-writer news, though, it's thanks to the cod-Celtic he used at the end of "Rats" that Lovecraft got a nitpicky letter from Robert E. Howard, and thus began their legendary correspondence and friendship.

9. Much as we saw words as the manifestation of, and theorized them as the entry-way for, the horror in "Statement of Randolph Carter."

proves himself able to master Poe's tools and move on—it serves as the solid foundation for his triumphant farewell to Poe, *Charles Dexter Ward*.

****

In my own case, reading this story also let all the light in at once about the "house as violated human body" subtext that, for example, William Hope Hodgson used in *House on the Borderland*. Indeed, "The Rats in the Walls" is a great, if somewhat over-loud, haunted house story as well—the comparisons with, say, *The Haunting of Hill House* or *The Shining* just jump out at you. It's instructive in this context to note Poe's dictum on locale:

> *[I]t has always appeared to me that a close circumscription of space is absolutely necessary to the effect of insulated incident—it has the force of a frame to a picture. It has an indisputable moral power in keeping concentrated the attention, and, of course, must not be confounded with mere unity of place.*

We can see Lovecraft apply this dictum in tales like "From Beyond," "The Temple," and "Erich Zann," as well as closer "haunted house" parallels such as "Picture in the House" and "The Shunned House." As the tales go on, though, the circumscribed spaces get vaster and more sublime: the underground warrens in this tale spread out to become vast buried gulfs in *At the Mountains of Madness* and "Shadow Out of Time," and a single circumscribed attic in "Dreams in the Witch House" turns out to contain all of hyperspace.

****

On a far more pointless note, the use of President Harding's death as a thematic sting just before Delapore's final descent may be unique in popular fiction. This is the sort of detail that just hangs there and niggles at me—did some unknown cadet Delapore kill Harding? Was President Harding somehow protecting the world against the Rats in its Walls? Yes, yes, I know it's just a weird thematic choice. And Roswell was a weather balloon, Buzzkill Bob.

****

For those of you running Elizabethan horror games, I'll note that the last Baron Exham, the heroic Walter De la Poer, discovers the awful truth about his family and flees Britain during "the reign of James the First." Surely you can do something with that, perhaps tied in with John Dee's researches into the ancient Welsh language, which of course the De la Poer basements would preserve...

****

This is also one of the few HPL stories to have anything like a typical roleplaying-game player-character investigator party in it. There's a dilettante, a former pilot, an archaeologist, an anthropologist, a cat, and a renowned psychic (with whose weak-minded powerlessness Lovecraft has a great deal of fun). They're even "bearing powerful electric searchlights and implements of excavation." No shotguns, though. Tch tch tch.

THE UNNAMABLE

[SEPTEMBER 1923]

This is a critical essay disguised (not particularly well) as a horror story, and like virtually all "message pieces," it's clumsy and not very interesting as a story. Lovecraft will write this same essay, and tell this same joke, again much more effectively in "Pickman's Model." Even as criticism, it isn't helped by the fact that Lovecraft in 1923 was still in the grip of puerile Decadent aesthetics, which clash badly with his Augustan tastes. Hence, like HPL's other literary-critical essay in the form of a mediocre story, "Celephaïs," it suffers from Lovecraft's essential unsuitedness for writing in the style he thought he should. (Compare, for example, the smooth confidence with which "Haunter of the Dark" demonstrates what we hear about Blake's aesthetic.) It does make one think that the various dialogues of Plato would be more riveting if the symposists might be attacked by ghost-monsters at any juncture, though.

As a pile of signifiers, tropes, and general stuff, the story is somewhat better—we see a little hint of the "suicide-by-philosophy" as Mary Sue Carter gets attacked by spectral awfuls, there's some pretty good use of genuine New England folklore (complete with unwarranted but admittedly effective slagging off on the Puritans), and George Wetzel insists that the story demonstrates that for Lovecraft ghosts are hideous and grotesque. This last provides a bit of a link between the supernatural unnamables of pre-HPL fiction and the alien unnamables of mature Lovecraft; it's probably worth a bit of chewing over.

Namelessness is another strong element in Lovecraft, beginning with the narrator of "Dagon" and, to hit only the high points, running through the pointedly nameless "Terrible Old Man" and "He," "The Nameless City," the indescribable (and hence impossible to name) "Colour Out of Space," and Wilbur Whateley's unnamed twin. The narrators of *At the Mountains of Madness* and "Shadow Over Innsmouth" are both unnamed in the stories, both the "Thing on the Doorstep" and "Shadow Out of Time" feature nameless entities possessing their narrators, and even the greatest name of all—Cthulhu—is explained as a mere approximation of the unspeakable.

THE FESTIVAL

[OCTOBER 1923]

This story always puts me in mind of eels, who migrate, transform, and die when it's time. Like the eel, our narrator feels an "ancestral call" to gather at a specific spot, in this case a vast cavern underneath Kingsport. (Which is itself a kind of architectural Sargasso, but that's pushing the metaphor.) Once there, he will undergo a metamorphosis that will change him forever and be unable to return to his normal life. Of course, this being a Lovecraft story, he panics instead and flings himself into the underground river (talk about your potent tropes—this one goes back to before the tales of Sinbad), where he washes up back in the "normal world." (Here, again, the connection with the apocalyptic "Dagon" and its unreliable narrator.)

He is the eel who woke up and saw himself trapped in his ancestry, trapped in an immense pattern he didn't create, and one that will easily survive his insignificant defection from it. In my reading, "The Festival" is Lovecraft's cosmic fatalism in miniature: all humanity is trapped in the patterns of entropy, evolution, and geology, to be destroyed by sudden unknowable catastrophe or erased in slow grinding erosion. The human who sees this clearly—the eel who wakes up—can't change it. The act of awakening, meanwhile, separates him from the rest of society.

****

Although I have to say that the Miskatonic University Library's policy of letting inmates at local insane asylums study the *Necronomicon* is probably not helping matters.

****

It's also interesting that in "The Festival," Lovecraft locates the center of the cosmic evil beneath Kingsport, which he based upon memories of a 1922 visit to the beautifully preserved colonial town of Marblehead, Mass. HPL described that visit as "the most powerful single emotional climax experienced during my nearly forty years of existence... That was the high tide of my life." Somehow, for Lovecraft, the act of perceiving his utopia simultaneously undermined it, perhaps by awakening his cosmic perception: as he put it, the sight "identified me with the stupendous totality of all things..."

UNDER THE PYRAMIDS

[FEBRUARY 1924]

[Originally published in Weird Tales *as "Imprisoned With the Pharaohs," which is how us old-school Lovecraftians grew up referring to it.]*

Lovecraft ghost-wrote this tale in February of 1924 for Harry Houdini, as a sales-building ploy for *Weird Tales*. (Walter Gibson, creator of the Shadow, may have ghost-written the other two "Houdini" stories published in *WT*.) Apparently Houdini liked it, which is more than I can say. S.T. Joshi and Lin Carter (whose generally good editorial taste shouldn't be confused with his less than stellar prose) agree with Houdini, so I guess you pays your money and you takes your chance.

Me, I think the whole thing reeks of a half-planned rush job padded out by desperate research-dumping, and believe me, I know one of those when I see it. Any hint of cosmicism in the end is drowned completely by the increasing hilarity of the narrative as Harry Houdini, our heroic narrator, continuously faints and swoons like a maiden aunt…or like a Lovecraft protagonist. (Joshi reads this as a "tart spoof." Mmm-hmm.) Lovecraft was absolutely correct when he wrote that he had little facility with the "action" genre, and this story proves it.

****

But Houdini and Lovecraft—there's a team-up! (They do team up in the novel *The Arcanum*, which I haven't yet read.) In honor of "Under the Pyramids," then, here's some half-digested research passed off as riveting narrative. (Much of this info comes from Chris Perridas' excellent 'Lovecraft and His Legacy' blog[10].)

- Lovecraft saw Houdini perform in Providence in 1898. HPL was eight years old.
- Lovecraft collaborated with/revised stories for C.M. Eddy, a ghostwriter for Houdini and one of Houdini's agents—Eddy and his family and circle of acquaintances gathered personal information for Houdini to use in fraudulent séance work (which Houdini did to expose mediums, of course).
- In November 1923, Lovecraft and Eddy wander around Chepachet, R.I., looking for the "Dark Swamp." They supposedly find nothing.

---

10. At **http://chrisperridas.blogspot.com/**

- HPL wrote the story for Houdini in February 1924, and met Houdini in person by September 1924. Houdini spent much of the fall of 1924 trying to work his connections to get Lovecraft a job.
- Houdini's book *A Magician Among the Spirits* appears in May 1924; he gives HPL an autographed copy: "To my friend, Howard Lovecraft / Best Wishes, / Houdini / "My brain is the key that sets me free."
- Lovecraft got tickets from Houdini for his show at the Hippodrome in New York for January 15, 1925.
- On February 1 (Candlemas, like I need to tell you that), 1925, H.P. Lovecraft and C.M. Eddy visited Houdini at midnight. The next day, Eddy and HPL had a dinner party at an Italian restaurant frequented by Houdini; Eddy then went to meet Houdini at the Hippodrome. The day after that, Houdini gave a "séance" to expose spirit mediums in New York.
- Cthulhu rises, per Lovecraft's story, between February 28 and April 2, 1925.
- Muriel Eddy recalls a dinner-date at the Waldorf with Lovecraft and Houdini on September 20, 1925 (I'm not sure if the date is from Muriel or Perridas), which she calls Houdini's last appearance in Providence. This might be the wrong year, as Houdini's last tour came through Providence on September 20, 1926.
- During that tour, Joshi speculates that Houdini commissioned another ghosted piece that HPL mentions in his letters, an article debunking astrology, which has not survived. Possibly as a result of that essay, Houdini, Eddy, and Lovecraft planned to collaborate on a general debunking book, *The Cancer of Superstition*.
- During the 1926 tour, Bess Houdini got food poisoning *in Providence*. At the dinner with Lovecraft? Did she eat something meant for HPL or her husband?
- Per DeCamp's biography, Houdini asked Lovecraft to meet him in Detroit to work on another article, debunking witchcraft. Before HPL could do so, Houdini had died (under murky circumstances,

with his appendix on the wrong side of his body) in Detroit, on Halloween, 1926.
- Also on Halloween, 1926, Lavinia Whateley vanishes, likely Assumed by Yog-Sothoth. (Justin Geoffrey and Richard Upton Pickman also die or vanish in 1926, no dates given.)

So...Lovecraft and Houdini—both New Yorkers at this time—hook up at midnight on Imbolc. Houdini carries out a fake séance—a protective ritual against Cthulhu's imminent (and immanent) rising? The next year, they are just about to start a major anti-occult campaign when first Bess is poisoned (in Providence!) and a month later Houdini dies unexpectedly of peritonitis (though DeCamp repeatedly refers to Houdini's death as "cancer"). On Halloween, while Yog-Sothoth is tangent to North America. Lovecraft backs off the project in public, but dies 11 years later, also of a multiply-diagnosed ailment of the renal area. I smell the spoor of the Black-Winged Ones, and perhaps a rascally Lascar or two.

THE SHUNNED HOUSE

[MID-OCTOBER 1924]

In "The Shunned House," Lovecraft can be seen gathering his legs beneath him for his mighty spring into greatness. It's not quite as pure as "Erich Zann," and not quite as powerful as "Rats in the Walls," but there's something in this story that stretches up past both of them toward the towering heights of "Call of Cthulhu," which HPL would write within a year and a half.

The rigorous scientism of the horror presages *At the Mountains of Madness* just as the rigorous historicality of the setting presages *Charles Dexter Ward*. ("Cthulhu" takes from both strands, but lightly.) With "The Shunned House," Lovecraft has assembled almost his entire mature repertoire of themes, effects, and methods—only the transcendence is missing, and this story is all the more impressive for its absence.

This despite the fact that its most notable overture toward cosmicism, the "titan elbow" of the thing in the basement, is just plain silly. Fortunately, the tremendous amount of scientific hugger-mugger Lovecraft deploys—mentions of relativity, quantum mechanics, lines of force, and so on—goes quite a way to cushion the blow. Indeed, the introduction of this scientific lore alongside with the (very authentic) ghost and werewolf lore collected in the earlier part of the story serves to emphasize the span of time between the primitive Huguenot vampire in the cellar and the present-day ghost-breaking Whipples, and to point up the multi-dimensional nature of the evil in the house.

I would go so far, contra Joshi (and contra Farnsworth Wright, who rejected "The Shunned House" when Lovecraft submitted it to *Weird Tales*) as to say that the slow, labored buildup of historical and spectral details and the equally dense justification that the modern, scientific Whipple narrator gives for the continuing horrors are both structurally necessary for the narrative (especially the pacing) to work correctly, and thematically necessary for the transmission of the exact weird sensation—of paranormality, not supernaturalism—that Lovecraft intends. It's not as able and seemingly effortless as some of Lovecraft's later work would usually be (although anyone who finds this story "dry and long-winded" with a "bathetic" ending, as Joshi claims to, shouldn't be as fond of "Shadow Out of Time" as Joshi claims he is), but it's much, much better than the critical consensus seems to have it.

****

As a little lagniappe, I'll note that "The Shunned House" conveys the horror of the "common soul" we've noted before, as the Roulet vampire imposes (or impinges) its "lines of force" on others in the house and finally absorbs Uncle Elihu into its "multitude" of faces. One could draw some interesting lines from this story toward Lovecraft's hatred of "mongrelization," his fear of the mass man (he wrote this story while still in New York), his strong distaste for social pressures from economics to editing to marriage, his concern with degeneration (expressed here, as in "Cool Air" and perhaps "Doorstep," as deliquescence), and even his architectural mysticism (like "Rats," the monster is in some real way congruent—sharing grue?—with the house, although the implication of parasitism is stronger than that of symbiosis), or his pride in materialist mechanism (implying an absence of individual souls) and in his Augustan-colonial tradition (a "line of force" shaping his outlook just as the dead hand of Roulet does the Harris family). You can just keep circling around and around, looking at Roulet as the past—still unnaturally present as with the Gothic, a survival of individual will that exists by breaking, deforming, and absorbing the will of others (Tradition), revealed through history and excavation (another metaphor for science—or for self-knowledge, if you like), and so on.

****

And dude, Whipple Jnr. armors up with flame-throwers, a "large and specially fitted Crookes tube," sulfuric acid, and a gas mask, and he burns out the evil despite fainting! He weeps at his uncle's death, but the ghost is well and truly broken, and we end with the happiest ending in all of Lovecraft: "The barren old trees in the yard have begun to bear small, sweet apples, and last year the birds nested in their gnarled boughs." Providence is cleansed; Eden prevails. What a great story.

THE HORROR AT RED HOOK

[AUGUST 1-2, 1925]

After reading this line:

He was conscious...that modern people under lawless conditions tend uncannily to repeat the darkest instinctive patterns of primitive half-ape savagery in their daily life and ritual observances...

I am reminded forcibly of John McTiernan's grossly under-rated early film *Nomads*. Well worth seeing, if you haven't.

The tale clearly owes a great debt to Machen, specifically (I'd say) "Novel of the Black Seal," along with (of course) "The Red Hand," which is where the epigraph comes from. Within the Mythos, it prefigures Ramsey Campbell's tales of urban alienation, and T.E.D. Klein's "Children of the Kingdom." At one remove, perhaps, F. Paul Wilson's *The Tomb* (and the Repairman Jack sequence that followed) can be seen as heirs of "Red Hook," as can Whitley Strieber's *Wolfen* and possibly even Dan Simmons' *Song of Kali*.

****

In a way, the most pulp of Lovecraft stories—one might say, the only pulp Lovecraft story. It features all the standard elements of weird adventure stories—evil foreigners, tunnels under the City, cribbed occult research, mysterious reversals of plot that get dropped as soon as the next scene is underway—with enough of the Lovecraftian cosmic to taste.

This doesn't, necessarily, make it a very good story, and considered purely from a structural viewpoint, Joshi and Cannon are right to dismiss it. For an intrepid detective, Malone doesn't actually do much, and the final action is just confused without accomplishing anything. It's also pretty inescapably drenched with Lovecraft's howling racism, unleashed after two years in Babylon-on-Hudson.

This is much, much more than the reflexive racism we often find in Lovecraft—the cat's name in "Rats in the Walls," for instance, or even the "nautical-looking Negro" in "Call of Cthulhu"—or in most any popular writer of the period (or in comic books and movies, among other pop-culture art forms, well into the 1960s and 1970s).

No, in "Red Hook" the racism is fully intentional, just like the romance is in "Romeo and Juliet." It's the entire theme of the story. The question becomes, what do we do about it? Certainly it's possible for an individual reader to be more repulsed than horrified by "Red Hook," just as it's possible for an individual reader to find nothing appealing about Juliet, but I think it's less-than-honest criticism to pretend that such is the inevitable effect of the story.

Because that sheer drive, to indict his neighbors for the crime of inspiring his hatred, makes the story just compelling reading, in much the same way that Sax Rohmer's Fu Manchu novels are. This is what happens when Lovecraft joins his eye for setting to a setting he simply despises; the power is unmistakable, even if (especially because, I'd say) the matter is unpleasant. Not for this story the arch rodomontades of "Cool Air," or the distant antiquarianism of "He." This is a story about New York, in the raw, if not cut remotely on our bias.

****

Are we entitled to dismiss horror on topics, and from perspectives, that we find objectionable? Obviously, we're entitled to read or not read whatever we wish. But it seems a little pecksniffy to dismiss some topics as not merely "not my cup of tea," but to attempt to read them out of the genre as essentially "too unpleasant for horror." In what sense, then, are we really interested in horror, if not in the transgressive power of it? I'm no more delighted with Lovecraft's "Arab with a hatefully negroid mouth" and the rest of that ugliness than I imagine most of you good people are, but it seems to me that if we consider real, urgent horror—the shock of cold water, the punch in the stomach, the sheer gut-wrench—to be a desideratum, we are cutting ourselves off if we say "Please, only give me horror that transgresses sexual boundaries I'm more titillated by than scared of" or "Please, only give me horror that transgresses categories set down by medieval Catholics I've never heard of and wouldn't give two hoots for if I had." Don't mistake my meaning: Caitlin Kiernan and Russell Kirk have produced some great, great horror tales, and their horrors are no less real for being less than universally shared, or even for appealing primarily to the conscience or the intellect, as they so often do. But it's also important for horror to, well, horrify, from the gut, and I think it's best when it such horror horrifies honestly, and as fully as possible.

This is urban horror. Swallow it, or move back to Providence.

****

That said, although I'm normally the one wishing for a better version of Lovecraft's more promising early tales, I'm (perhaps hypocritically, by my own indictment) just as glad that he never reworked this particular vein of urban horror into a true masterpiece.

HE

[AUGUST 10-11, 1925]

"He" is another example of Lovecraft's preferring, even privileging, incident over action in weird fiction. It's very like "Nyarlathotep," albeit with a merely personal apocalypse at the coda of the general one revealed in the windows. There are also structural and topical similarities to "Erich Zann," including the sorcerous window, the musical theme (it's the hellish music of the future that drives our narrator mad), and the insistence on silence during the revelation.

****

"He" is firmly, inextricably rooted in New York history and topography—like many other great ghost stories, it's about a place more than it is anything else. Hence, this is one of those stories I had to re-read after leaving Oklahoma City in order to fully appreciate it. For me, Chicago is Lovecraft's New York and Lovecraft's Providence in one. This passage, in particular, is exactly how Chicago hit me when I first crossed the Michigan Avenue bridge:

> *I had seen it in the sunset from a bridge, majestic above its waters, its incredible peaks and pyramids rising flowerlike and delicate from pools of violet mist to play with the flaming clouds and the first stars of evening. Then it had lighted up window by window above the shimmering tides where lanterns nodded and glided and deep horns bayed weird harmonies, and had itself become a starry firmament of dream, redolent of faery*

music, and one with the marvels of Carcassonne and Samarcand and El Dorado and all glorious and half-fabulous cities.

For me, then, "He" is a profoundly true story. However, I differ from Lovecraft's narrator, or perhaps Chicago differs from New York:

I saw at last a fearful truth which no one had ever dared to breathe before—the unwhisperable secret of secrets—the fact that this city of stone and stridor is not a sentient perpetuation of Old New York as London is of Old London and Paris of Old Paris, but that it is in fact quite dead, its sprawling body imperfectly embalmed and infested with queer animate things which have nothing to do with it as it was in life.

One of the many wonderful, terrifying things about Chicago is the degree to which Chicago is, indeed, a sentient perpetuation of its past.

Not that Chicago doesn't have its "imperfectly embalmed" bits, too.

****

The description of Lovecraftian magic in this tale is one of the best:

To—my ancestor...there appeared to reside some very remarkable qualities in the will of mankind; qualities having a little-suspected dominance not only over the acts of one's self and of others, but over every variety of force and substance in Nature, and over many elements and dimensions deemed more universal than Nature herself.

It is my profound hope that between "He" and "Dreams in the Witch House" it will be possible to determine just what Lovecraftian sorcery is good for besides summoning things that will eat you.

Not that there's anything wrong with that.

****

Joshi, at least, thinks there might be a shoggoth foreshadowed there at the end: "a colossal, shapeless influx of inky substance starred with shining, malevolent eyes," although the story makes it fairly clear that it is the vengeance-spirit (the ghastly soul-symbol?) of the "half-breed red Indians" coming after the squire. (But see Robert Waugh and China Miéville for differing interpretations of the shoggoth as Semitic horde or urban lumpenproletariat.) This is not one of those stories that particularly refutes Lovecraft's racism, although he interestingly borrows from Poe by describing the squire as "too white."

****

As I've mentioned in my collection of Mythos miscellanea, ***Dubious Shards***, I basically agree with Houellebecq's assessment of "He" as Lovecraft's autobiographical rejection letter to New York City. This is probably where I should grudgingly admit that H.P. Lovecraft would likely have made himself miserable in Chicago, if he'd taken the offer to become editor of *Weird Tales* in March of 1924. He certainly would have hated the weather, and sad to say, he might well have been blind to the glories of Chicago architecture. But still... Competent editing for *Weird Tales*! Lovecraft in Chicago! If only ...

IN THE VAULT

[SEPTEMBER 18, 1925]

This is Lovecraft's last truly bad story, and it's one of his worst. Even Lovecraft's language, which normally has its delights even in the most tiresome moments, is seemingly purposely flat and bald while still wrapped around an interminable series of narrative switchbacks. The setting is nowhere, and there aren't even any of those weird Lovecraftian bits that make you wish he'd written a different story that day. Nope, this is a day you wish he'd written a long, whiny letter to his aunts about those bastard Syrians next door, or maybe just spent the day inventing new spellings for "foetor" or patronizingly explaining Nietzsche to Frank Belknap Long.

Do me a favor: You get a time machine, you go back to September 18, 1925, you knock on Lovecraft's door and say "Hey, they're giving away free ice cream at this place on Sixth and Ninety-Third to anyone who can name all of Hawthorne's novels!" Then you can go off and kill Hitler or whatever, satisfied with a job well done.

Seriously, Al Feldstein would have been embarrassed to write somthing this pointless on deadline day for *Tales From the Crypt* in 1953. "Too obvious," he'd say. "Just run a house ad or something." And he'd be right.

Cool Air

[February 1926]

An innocuous piece of urban horror:

> *It is a mistake to fancy that horror is associated inextricably with darkness, silence, and solitude. I found it in the glare of mid-afternoon, in the clangour of a metropolis, and in the teeming midst of a shabby and commonplace rooming-house...*

"Cool Air" is good, but not great, a story from the Machen-Stevenson "Baghdad-on-the-Thames" (or in this case, "-Hudson") tradition. I disagree with Joshi and Cannon, who rank it above Lovecraft's other urban-horror tale, "The Horror at Red Hook." I liked it better, as the man says, when it was called "Facts in the Case of M. Valdemar" or "The Novel of the White Powder."

****

I'm fairly sure that Lovecraft was having his little joke when he describes Dr. Muñoz as "obviously of superior blood," given what we later find out about the good doctor's blood. This brings up the possibility that he contrasts Dr. Muñoz intentionally with, and thus purposely denigrates, the other lodgers, "mostly Spaniard a little above the coarsest and crudest grade." The same can be said of the contrast between Muñoz' cultured Lovecraftian tones with the stereotyped diction of the landlady, Mrs. Herrero. I'm not sure if it makes it better, or worse, that HPL is consciously using racial or ethnic stereotypes to improve his fiction, and that it works.

****

Note that we have entered the realm of the dead—not just the cold, but the "room smelled like a vault of a sepulchred Pharaoh in the Valley of Kings." Note that workmen and laborers (what HPL would no doubt consider "the lower orders") instinctively fear the doctor, just as animals do a vampire or werewolf. In the absence of animal life, Lovecraft (and other writers of urban fantasy or horror) need some sort of spoor denoting a disturbance of the natural order.

Because Muñoz is not merely a scientist, but a magus. Just as alchemists used highly technical equipment in magical pursuits, so the doctor uses not just "an absorption system of ammonia cooling" and "a scientific enhancement of will and consciousness" (mesmerism? psychic powers?) but "exotic spices and Egyptian incense," and "the incantations of the mediaevalists." We have another note about how Lovecraftian magic functions:

> [H]e believed these cryptic formulae to contain rare psychological stimuli which might conceivably have singular effects on the substance of a nervous system from which organic pulsations had fled.

We're more than halfway to the Essential Saltes already.

****

And just what awesome story hooks lie under this section?

> He acquired a habit of writing long documents of some sort, which he carefully sealed and filled with injunctions that I transmit them after his death to certain persons whom he named—for the most part lettered East Indians, but including a once celebrated French physician now generally thought dead, and about whom the most inconceivable things had been whispered.

And this is just an *average* Lovecraft story.

The Call of Cthulhu

[Plotted August 12-13, 1925; written August 1926]

The first and the simplest emotion which we discover in the human mind is Curiosity.
  — Edmund Burke, *A Philosophical Enquiry Into the Origin of Our Ideas on the Sublime and Beautiful*

The oldest and strongest emotion of mankind is fear, and the oldest and strongest kind of fear is fear of the unknown.
  — H.P. Lovecraft, *Supernatural Horror In Literature*

The story "The Call of Cthulhu" is essentially about the collision between these two first lines, these two truths, from its own immortal first line about the merciful failure of human comprehension to almost the last: "A time will come—but I must and cannot think!" Curiosity—the "piecing together of dissociated knowledge"—causes terror. The fear of the unknown drives us to investigate it, revealing that the truth is even worse. In Lovecraft's epistemology, just like his mythology, we begin and end with fear and loathing.

Lovecraft wrote from the Gothic tradition, but for the twentieth century; the threat to order isn't villainous, swarthy Catholics (although …) but the actual circumstances of reality. Lovecraft has taken all the core Gothic tropes—the alien (but powerful) Outsider, the threat of miscegenation, the inevitably corrupt ancient wisdom, the symptomatic disorder of Nature, the "haunted castle" or ruin, even the insipid hero, and—often literally—enlarged upon them. Made them vaster. And brought them out of the "shudder tale" and into the world of science, and hence into science fiction. For Lovecraft, the Gothic ruin is the universe, and vice versa. Reality—Rutherford's primordial rocks and Shapley's unimaginably vast (and hence ancient) cosmos—is itself the dead, "Gothic" survival intruding on our transient joys. Discovering that, seeing the huge ruins in which we dwell (and beneath which we will decay and become as nothing) is the climax, the anagnorisis, the "big reveal." As Stefan Dziemianowicz puts it, "The unique effect he reaches for here is not so much fright, but a sort of intellectual shock." But where in a standard Gothic, we ease the tension, punish the villain, and marry the couple off, Lovecraft ends the action with the villains uncompromisingly in charge—"forget about it, Jake, it's R'lyeh."

In short, Lovecraft is working the Burkean Sublime for all he's worth. Note that this could be either because Burke is right about the Sublime, or because Lovecraft was a Burkean. Honesty compels me to admit that as far as I can determine, Lovecraft doesn't seem to have owned a copy of Burke, and he doesn't mention his aesthetics in the *Selected Letters* or *Supernatural Horror*, but I refuse to believe that the conservative horrorist HPL never read Burke's *Enquiry*.

Burke says, essentially, that the Sublime is different from the Beautiful, arising in not love and delight but in fear (especially the fear of death): "Terror is in all cases whatsoever, either more openly or latently the ruling principle of the Sublime." The Sublime manifests in (or is materially caused by) such aspects or concepts as vastness, infinity, obscurity, and power. Burke notes qualities such as unfinishedness (or ruination), magnitude, difficulty or impossibility, and even "sad and fuscous colours" as symptomatic of the Sublime. Sound familiar yet?

Another quote from Burke's *Enquiry* to seal the deal:

> *The passion caused by the great and sublime in nature...is Astonishment; and astonishment is that state of the soul, in which all its motions are suspended, with some degree of horror. In this case the mind is so entirely filled with its object, that it cannot entertain any other.*

This Astonishment is one of the effects, of course, of seeing Cthulhu, whether in dreams or (as the unfortunate Johansen did) awake. Even language becomes deranged—Lovecraft repeatedly resorts to seemingly weak similes and metaphors to describe Cthulhu or R'lyeh. ("A mountain walked or stumbled.") This is not because Lovecraft is a weak writer, but because describing Cthulhu is supposed to be sheerly impossible—the mind keeps asymptotically shooting off before it can fully connect. (This is also the role played by all that "non-Euclidean geometry"—R'lyeh is simultaneously unfinished and ruined, ever-changing and extra-dimensional, too Sublime for comprehension within Reason.) Robert M. Price is fond of calling the Lovecraft Mythos an "anti-mythology"—this, then, is anti-scripture. It's scripture that does not reveal the Divine, but cloak it. It even ends with the opposite of an evangelist Call—Thurston urges his heirs to destroy the manuscript rather than promulgate it. Just as the divine Word of infinite meaning, the LOGOS, begins Creation, the anti-LOGOS of infinite un-meaning, "*Cthulhu fhtagn*," ends it. But creepily, "*Cthulhu fhtagn*" also begins each testament of the tale, sparking the Creation (of the sculpture) in Wilcox' dream, revealing itself as Prophecy in the cries of the Louisiana bayou cultists inspiring Legrasse to track their theology down, and (inferentially) announcing itself in the dreams of the "Kanakas and half-castes" (the Magi?) that the *Alert* accidentally intercepts in the South Pacific on their way to the Nativity/Incarnation.

And yes, Burke notes that the Divine is a lot more Sublime, at least as we experience it, than it is Beautiful.

****

I haven't even touched on the brilliantly complex, almost archaeological structure of the story, how it formally recapitulates its own telling by piecing together seemingly unrelated narratives, with Thurston almost vanishing into transparency as a reader-surrogate.

****

Or mentioned the weird black-winged things in the Louisiana swamp that "Old Castro" claims did all the actual killing for the Cult.

****

But instead I'll close with another observation lifted from Stefan Dziemianowicz. The three sub-narrators in the tale recapitulate previous

Lovecraftian protagonists. The sculptor Wilcox is a "neurotic and excited" Poe-narrator as found in "The Hound," "Hypnos," and so forth. Inspector Legrasse is a tough-minded adventurer in the mold of Harley Warren, Harry Houdini, Detective Malone, the junior Whipple from "The Shunned House," and the quester "for strange horrors in literature and life" from "The Lurking Fear." Finally, the sailor Johansen is a blend of the narrators of "Dagon" and "The Temple" (sailors who come to misadventure) with the narrator of "The Nameless City" (someone who explores a ruin in the distant waste). As Dziemianowicz puts it:

> *Lovecraft seems to be commenting subtly on his previous work, saying that none of his earlier approaches to horror fiction is as powerful as the [vaster] new one that embraces all three.*

Note that Thurston, who assembles all three perspectives into a master (monster?) narrative, is Lovecraft's first purely academic narrator, and will be far from the last.

PICKMAN'S MODEL

[September 1926]

> *I can shew you a house [Cotton Mather] lived in, and I can shew you another one he was afraid to enter in spite of all his fine bold talk!*
> — RICHARD UPTON PICKMAN

This is pretty much the core of "Pickman's Model," where history meets fear and legend, again rooted to a setting drawn with almost Pickman-like realism. Joshi is excellent where he notes that Pickman's expressed aesthetics in painting are the same as Lovecraft's in fiction. Note, by the way, the immense improvement over not quite six years between this work and "Celephaïs," also about a rejected artist who winds up carried into an Otherworld, also intended as artistic "criticism of the deed."

However, I confess that my absolute favorite parts of the story are the descriptions of Pickman's pictures, especially "Subway Accident" (which is really just terrifying, implying some degree of official cooperation, at least in a cover-up of the ghoul infestation) and the Bierce-ian black joke of "Holmes, Lowell, and Longfellow Lie Buried In Mount Auburn." In the latter you can almost see Lovecraft's wry smile as the provincial Providence man takes lit'ry Boston Brahminism down several notches.

Methinks Robert Bloch agreed with me—his magnificent novel *Strange Eons* opens with the protagonist discovering "Ghoul Feeding" in an old antique shop.

The story, in short, is excellent, and although I agree with Joshi that Lovecraft doesn't quite carry off Thurber's "hard-boiled" voice, I think it's at most a minor flaw in a nearly perfected collage of horror, history, allusion, art-criticism, and black, bleak humor.

THE STRANGE HIGH HOUSE IN THE MIST

[NOVEMBER 9, 1926]

By the way, I'm almost forgetting to mention 'The Strange High House in the Mist', which impressed me with renewed power. It is like an eyrie from which the imagination can take flight to 'worlds of undiscovered gold'.

— CLARK ASHTON SMITH,
LETTER TO H.P. LOVECRAFT, MARCH 11 1930

If anything, this note of Smith's is an understatement. The estimable John Rateliff calls "Strange High House" Lovecraft's "single best story," which is going a trifle too far in my opinion, but it's certainly HPL's single best fantasy story, better even than "Sarnath" or "Cats of Ulthar," not least because it has a complexity and a multi-dimensionality not usually found in Lovecraft's fantasies—and not in his horror tales until *At the Mountains of Madness* or thereabouts.

"The Call of Cthulhu," a truly great story, is by contrast essentially a dizzying, vertiginous fugue in one direction—"vastness" or "sublimity" or what-have-you. Every note, from every source, comes back to the same chords. But in "Strange High House" we have two dimensions working—Thomas Olney's quest for something Other, which in Lovecraft's "Dunsanian" tales is usually a noble thing (even a smugly noble thing, pace "Celephaïs"), and the impingement of the Other on the town of Kingsport, which begins in standard Lovecraftian spook-mode as dangerous, then seemingly joins up with the "noble quest" in a reversal. Except that Olney comes down "hollow," and the Kingsporters fear that the old gods have renewed their appetite for questers. Lovecraft, in other words, is endorsing Olney's quest—there is a nobler, higher, altogether better truth Outside—while condemning it—such quests bring the Outside closer and will hollow out first Kingsport and then perhaps all the world. We end with a kind of photo-negative of Machen's "Great Return," or an echo of Eliot's words: "Mankind cannot bear too much reality." Kingsport becomes Semele, beloved of the gods and burnt alive by their regard.

And on a sheerly mechanical level, there's almost not a word out of place; Lovecraft almost effortlessly pulls aside the curtain on Erich Zann's window to show us where our world and Outside are tangent: "And it was very odd that shingles so worm-eaten could survive, or bricks so crumbled still form a standing chimney." Only the actual immanence of the gods seems anticlimactic—Neptune is very much out of place, and even Nodens seems more like a courtly aristocrat than, you know, a god from the Abyss.

I can sort of see where he was going with it, of course. Lovecraft strongly differentiates between Neptune and Nodens as part of his "tension and release" method in this story. After the increasing creepiness of the climb (tension), Olney meets the House-keeper and is pleasantly invited in (release). We go through a couple more minor cycles of that and then the House-keeper gets hinky again (tension) but it's released with "Trident-bearing Neptune" (all very classical and clear), who is associated with words like "golden flames" and "sportive tritons and fantastic nereids." But the release is too stuttery, as when we get to the very next line, by contrast, Nodens is the "grey and awful form of primal Nodens, Lord of the Great Abyss," and even the nereids get weird with their gongs made of "grotesque resonant shells of unknown lurkers in black sea-caves" and we're back up to the tension.

But then "wizened" and "hoary" Nodens "helps" Olney and the Housekeeper into his shell and suddenly seems like a nice old guy with mobility issues. And too soon to really turn the corner—*wham!*—we cut away to Kingsport again. Neptune's introduction, and Nodens' sudden gentility, are both stutters toward release that don't quite work. I think it's because here's where the gears are meshing most finely between "noble dream-quest" and "terrible Faustian bargain."

Either Lovecraft should have reined in the awfulness for a pure "release" moment, presenting the gods' human face, or the Mighty Ones should have *both* been mixtures of the creepy and familiar.

And even if it doesn't quite work at that delicate moment of counterpoise, Lovecraft still effectively sets us up for the big sting at the end—one of the few true "surprise endings" in his whole oeuvre. That Nodens, what a nice guy. Maybe he'll come back more often. And drain the light out of everyone's eyes, the better to illuminate the high house in the mist.

THE DREAM-QUEST OF UNKNOWN KADATH

[OCTOBER 1926-JANUARY 22, 1927]

Despite its novella length (38,000 words), this novel—a literal phantasmagoria—is so rich, so meandering, so surprising, so tonally discordant, so clever, and so unrelieved in its flumes of incident and invention that it would take at least another 38,000 words to perform anything like an adequate critical examination.

So far, critics have pretty much confined themselves either to discovering its various antecedents (besides the obvious Dunsany tales "Idle Days on the Yann" and "Time and the Gods" again) or adumbrating on its main (and equally obvious) theme. George Wetzel apparently believes that the whole thing is a lengthy gloss on the *Aeneid*, which has the virtue of being strange enough to be plausible. Peter Cannon's theory that it is an Augustan *Vathek* is probably more sound, but there are further unmistakable parallels—if not influences—from Burroughs (alien hero—named Carter no less—fights a collection of ethnic stereotypes and Orientalist imagery in a nonsensical fantasyland) to Baum ("There's no place like home") to Burton (J. Vernon Shea believes that *Arabia Deserta* and other such travel narratives clearly influenced the novel) to Bunyan (one of Lovecraft's original titles for the novel was *A Pilgrim in Dreamland*), and that's only the 'B's. I suspect that a lot of it is that all quest tales will turn out to be strongly formally similar (like virtually all heroes of classical and Renaissance romance, for instance, Carter is kidnapped by pirates), though I wouldn't rule out anything Lovecraft proveably read. The re-imagining of his various "Dunsanian" locales and characters (including the heretofore non-"Dunsanian" Pickman, Nyarlathotep, Leng, and Randolph Carter himself) as all part of one "Dreamland" indicates that HPL was in jackdaw mode when he wrote *Dream-Quest*, which he soon considered mere "useful practice" for a real novel.

As far as the theme goes, it's (as I said) obvious: Carter realizes that the true city of wonder is Boston. Like so many of the "Dreamland" stories, *Dream-Quest* turns out to be about nothing so much as aesthetics. Lovecraft is turning away from the puerile Decadence he exalted in "Celephaïs" toward his own more natural metier of hyper-realism. This is a fond and final hail and farewell to "Dunsanian" thought (though Joshi argues that Lovecraft is not so much rejecting Dunsany as he is rejecting Lovecraft's own flawed view of Dunsany) and it not coincidentally also marks Lovecraft's joyous return to golden New England after fleeing the gug-infested canyons of New York City.

****

In my experience, readers either love *Dream-Quest* to bursting or they don't quite get the point. I tend toward the latter; the luxury of the novel form (and the absence, unlike *Charles Dexter Ward*, of any narrative layers or complexity) gives Lovecraft way too much space to thrash about stylistically. Although by 1926 he was just too good a writer to produce sheer endless waffle, I always feel like reading the thing straight through is a bit much of a muchness. (A surfeit of Turkish Delight, as it were.) As a result, by the time I get to the end, I'm never quite sure whether the "mild gods of Earth" are actually off in Boston, or in some sort of pocket-Boston, or if Nyarlathotep is just lying and the gods are dead, or what. (Keeping in mind the situation in "Time and the Gods"—in which Time destroys the gods' pleasure-dome—and what we've seen of the "mild gods of Earth" in "Strange High House in the Mist," none of these options sound particularly good for Hub City.) That said, there are some great, great incidents—the war of the Cats of Ulthar vs. the Cats of Saturn; the bravura episode with the Veiled Priest; the forest of the Zoogs; the sheer delight of meeting Pickman and realizing that, in Dreamland at least, the ghouls are all right.

The Silver Key

[early November 1926]

A very strange story, one that goes farther than any other, I think, to explicate just who Lovecraft thought he was, and a good bit of why he thought that. Why dredge through "The Outsider" for murky wracks of the Lovecraftian subconscious when he dissects his whole thought and philosophy for you right here? That said, it's hard to find this celebration of the urge to regress to childhood (as opposed to the past in general, or as opposed to the terrors of regression along the family tree) anywhere else in the canon (except, obviously, for *Dream-Quest*, written at the same time), and one is tempted to chalk that up to Lovecraft's brief, intense reaction to returning home to Providence after his nerve-shattering experience of "the pest zone" that was New York City.

Sadly, "The Silver Key" is so concerned with meticulously exploring Lovecraft/Carter's interior life and thought that it doesn't do much as a story; one understands why the readers of *Weird Tales* "heartily disliked" it. My reaction isn't as strong, but it is telling, I think, that I've re-read "From Beyond" (a far inferior piece of technical work on every level) probably six or seven times for every time I've read "Silver Key." It's not even the essential absence of plot: not much more happens in "From Beyond" on a story level either, but it lays out Lovecraft's cosmic dread far more compellingly than "Silver Key" does his "indifferentism." Plus, of course, even Lovecraft didn't believe that "the oldest and strongest emotion of mankind" is apathy, which is why there's a thriving horror literature, and tales of ennui are rapidly forgotten, *dei gratia*. Contrariwise, if you're a John Updike fan, maybe this is your favorite Lovecraft tale ever.

****

But "The Silver Key" is a guide to Lovecraft's thought only as far as November of 1926, and I think it's a fading guide even by then. Surely the ending of *Dream-Quest* (which becomes, unbelievably, a prequel to this story) rejects it already—it is not dream cities Carter searches for, but earthly Boston. It is my contention that Lovecraft must have changed his mind, at least aesthetically, even while he was finishing *Dream-Quest* in January of 1927—note his sudden lack of interest in the novel—and that *Charles Dexter Ward* (begun immediately after completing *Dream-Quest*) is almost his own response to it. Here we have a slew of characters, none of them remotely "indifferent," none of them Randolph Carter; a story in which the urge to regress takes on a historical tone—and resumes HPL's old horrifying tenor—that would inform almost every tale to follow. Even indifferentism becomes horrible, in "Colour Out of Space" and in the uncaring experimentations of fungoid Outer Ones and crinoid Elder Things. In a very real sense, then, almost everything truly lasting and important about Lovecraft's fiction emphatically rejects this story.

THE CASE OF CHARLES DEXTER WARD

[JANUARY 23-MARCH 1, 1927]

Again, I find that the better the story, the less I feel the need to say much else about it. Lovecraft himself sums up the novel, and indeed almost his whole oeuvre, in it, when Ward writes:

> *I have brought to light a monstrous abnormality, but I did it for the sake of knowledge. Now for the sake of all life and Nature you must help me thrust it back into the dark again.*

That, and the rapturous regionalism of the whole piece ("It was twilight, and Charles Dexter Ward had come home.") are clearly the fundamental thematic concerns, just as the formal structure of the piece is easily typed as a Poe-style detective story.

The novel is rich enough, of course, that you can chase any number of leitmotivs through it, from Lovecraft's use of his own autobiography to create the idealized Ward, to the eerie and continuous foregrounding of the visual senses (painting and architecture recur specifically, but there's a lot of explicitly visual description for HPL here) and their contrast with hidden lore, the clever uses of parallelisms to imply a cyclic "myth of Return" throughout, and the sheer excellence of Lovecraft's portrayal of Joseph Curwen's character. Curwen is far and away the best villain in Lovecraft—Wilbur Whateley is too pathetic, Asenath Waite is too camp, Herbert West is but a bravura cartoon, and the rest are deliberately opaque—and he withstands comparison with almost any other horror villain as well, up to and including Hannibal Lecter or Randall Flagg.

One productive vein to work in *Charles Dexter Ward* is the "Eden myth" of Lovecraft's utopian, antiquarian Providence with Curwen as its Serpent (both past and present) and Ward as its Adam. Joshi makes the very interesting point that in the great Providence tales—this novel, "Shunned House," and

"Haunter of the Dark"—the evil is defeated. Eden prevails. On the "Eden" theme, I will also indulge myself in a quote from Barton St. Armand:

> *If, according to the Christian tradition man is both lost and saved in a garden—Eden and Gethsemane—then according to Lovecraft's mythology man is both lost and saved in a library.*

There are, of course, lots of weird little loose ends: Why were Curwen, Orne, et al. planning to re-animate Ben Franklin of all people? Was the revenant from Number 118 Merlin or something even less human? What's with the werewolf sightings? And perhaps most insistent of all, why is resurrecting zombie savants (a relatively harmless activity as Lovecraftian hobbies go) threatening to "all life and Nature"? This sort of thing makes for great game fodder, even though most of it is probably down to the fact that the novel we have is a first draft at best, assembled (by Derleth and Wandrei) from a number of draft chapters sent around to Lovecraft's correspondence circle. Joshi reports we have an A.M.S. of "Ward," but I don't know if that refers to an intact original, or to the re-assembled postmortem text from which *Weird Tales* printed the novel in 1941.

****

Which is perhaps the most frightening thing, to me at any rate, about this piece. A (patchwork?) first draft, written in well under two months in 1927 and abandoned wrongly and foolishly by the author, is the *second-greatest horror novel of all time.* (Lovecraftian italics very much intentional.) Admittedly, at 50,000 words, it's not a very long novel, but horror needs a bit of confinement. The mind reels at how good a novel, and perhaps how many more years of Lovecraft's life, he and we were cheated of by HPL's "renunciation" of this work. It sat in pieces in his files or wherever for the next decade, while *four separate publishers* asked him if he had a novel they could see. Talk about lost and saved in a library.

****

Oh, all right. *Dracula, The Case of Charles Dexter Ward, The Haunting of Hill House, The Strange Case of Dr Jekyll and Mr Hyde, The Damnation Game, Carrion Comfort, The Ceremonies, Conjure Wife, The Boats of the 'Glen Carrig'*, and either *Declare* or *It*, depending on whether you count *Declare* as horror. (Conversely, I suppose, if you count *Heart of Darkness* as horror under the meaning of the act, then *Dracula* drops to number two and so forth.) I'm open to intelligent disputation on Nos. 5-10, although if you take off my choices for Barker, Simmons, and Hodgson, you're just going to wind up replacing them with *Cabal, Song of Kali*, and *House on the Borderland*, so why bother?

To allay the squawking I hear right now: *Frankenstein* is an important, vital, seminal novel that just isn't particularly good, even by the standards of early Romantic novels. Certain parts of it are brilliant, as is the overall thrust and theme. It's great literature, but only a mediocre novel.

THE COLOUR OUT OF SPACE

[MARCH 1927]

Lovecraft considered "The Colour Out of Space" to be his best story. I agree. I would rank it up there with "The Willows" and "The White People" and a handful of M.R. James ghost-stories as a perfect weird tale.

****

I believe I was reading a long, stodgy review of a biography of Melville when I ran across the following Melville quote, which has ever since been a major touch-stone of mine for the cosmic:

> *No country will more quickly dissipate romantic expectations than Palestine, particularly Jerusalem. To some, the disappointment is heart-sickening. Is the desolation of the land the result of the fatal embrace of the Deity? Hapless are the favorites of heaven.*

Now, while I obviously don't actually believe this to be the case, my Calvinist depths vibrate strongly to this particular chord. This, for me, is the purest form of cosmic horror, what Lovecraft summed up as the "idiot god Azathoth," or what Tim Powers evokes with the djinn in *Declare*— an intelligence so foreign, so inaccessible, that it can only appear mad or idiotic to us despite its immensity. (Like the "colour," its method cannot be perceived by human experience.) While researching my column on "Herne the Hunter" for *Suppressed Transmission*, I ran across Henry James, Sr., and his "vastation" at Windsor:

> [S]uddenly in a lightning-flash as it were "fear came upon me, and trembling, which made all my bones to shake." To all appearance it was a perfectly insane and abject terror, without ostensible cause, and only to be accounted for, to my perplexed imagination, by some damned shape squatting invisible to me within the precincts of the room, and raying out from his fetid personality influences fatal to life. The thing had not lasted ten seconds before I felt myself a wreck, that is, reduced from a state of firm, vigorous, joyful manhood to…an ever-growing tempest of doubt, anxiety, and despair…

This "vastation," I maintain (contra Swedenborg), is the Sublime spoor of Azathoth. Echoes of it occur in that great scene in *Gojira*, when the scientists discover a trilobite smashed into Gojira's footprint; you also get a diminuendo of a Sublime vastation in the 1951 version of *The Thing*, when the scientists back up and the camera pulls back to reveal the outline of an enormous crashed saucer under the ice.

****

Which brings up a point that occurred to me while I was listening to a reading from this story at the H.P. Lovecraft Ice Cream Social that 57th Street Books held to commemorate the 70th anniversary of Lovecraft's death. Namely, that this story, published in 1927, can be seen as a kind of tipping-point in cultural signifiers. If you'll forgive me getting all Northrop Frye on you, in the old medieval Christian tradition (and even the late Classical era) of stories, a visitor from Heaven was predominantly a good thing—a god or angel or saint. The figure I'll call "the brightly-colored stranger" was predominantly a bad thing—a lamia or devil or Pied Piper or Heathcliff. At some point, those signifiers switched.

Yes, H.G. Wells' alien invader predates HPL's. But it seems to me that Wells was doing something revolutionary, but that after 1930 or so—after 1927—any alien on earth was more likely to be an invader than not. Right now, if you go to a movie, knowing nothing about it, if it begins with a meteorite falling to Earth, it's 90% likely to be a horror movie. (Likewise, our modern myth of visitors from the sky, the Roswell Mythos, is a maltheist one straight outta Lovecraft.) If it begins with a brightly-colored stranger coming to town, it's almost as likely to be a romantic comedy. The brightly colored stranger is now the redeemer. (Which is why Roma Downey or Michael Landon's angel figures always walked into town, and didn't fall from the sky.) Sometimes, it "redeems" a whole family, or a whole town—whether they like it or not.

Hence, you can watch the film *Pleasantville*, for example, as a photographic negative of "The Colour Out of Space." As the color which nobody in the world has ever seen before spreads, their society is destroyed. We have met the Colour, and it is us.

THE DUNWICH HORROR

[AUGUST 1928]

Melodrama is undeniably present, and coincidence is stretched to a length which appears absurd upon analysis; but in the malign witchery of the tale as a whole these trifles are forgotten...

— H.P. LOVECRAFT ON "THE GREAT GOD PAN" BY ARTHUR MACHEN

This story is a bigger puzzle than it appears, since its immense popularity and undeniable effect stand squarely athwart the Higher Lovecraftian Criticism. To wit: It's a story of good vs. evil, in which good wins. This is nearly unforgiveable to critics like S.T. Joshi and Donald Burleson. The latter has even gone so far as to claim that "The Dunwich Horror" is self-parody, which Joshi correctly rejects on the face of it. Joshi simply thrashes around the story, unable to understand why Lovecraft's apparent abandoning of the supposed philosophical core of his work produced such a successful Lovecraft story.

Joshi even tries to deny its success, but his criticisms are either misplaced or wrong-headed. He calls Henry Armitage unrealistically pompous, although one would imagine that S.T. Joshi has met even more tenured academics than I have. He questions the use of the Powder of Ibn-Ghazi, which seems to have no purpose except to make the Horror visible, although it's apparent enough from Armitage's lectures that the Horror can only be destroyed ("split up into what it was originally made of") if a sufficient portion exists in our universe to be affected by the rites. Joshi also questions Old Whateley's prediction that "yew folks'll hear a child o' Lavinny's a-callin' its father's name on the top o' Sentinel Hill," saying that it serves only as "purportedly clever foreshadowing," when it's obvious that Whateley is performing the role of prophet (Simeon in the Temple, if you will), seemingly predicting one thing—the successful summoning of Yog-Sothoth by Wilbur and the concomitant end of the world—while tragically predicting his own son's death. Just that prophetic element alone, tying as it does Christian parallelism (which we'll come to anon) and Greek tragic construction with a touch of Shakespearean malice, is one of the single best bits in all of Lovecraft, and it bespeaks an alarming (and unusual) failure of Joshi's critical faculty that he apparently can't get it. The same applies, almost as intensely, to Joshi's insistence that the distancing of the climactic ritual (we see "three tiny figures" and hear only the natives' narration of the events) is comical rather than of a piece with almost every other Lovecraft story. He even cavils at HPL's blending of the countryside around Wilbraham and that around Athol to create "Dunwich," when again it's what Lovecraft has done with all his fictional places. In short, Joshi just can't take the contradiction between Lovecraft's "mechanist materialism" and the heroic, almost salvific, narrative of the story.

****

Joshi is correct, meanwhile, to point up the strong similarities between "The Dunwich Horror" and "The Great God Pan," to which Lovecraft even calls attention in the text. Robert M. Price further notes borrowings in this story from "The White People" (especially the diaries) and "The Novel of the Black Seal" with its goatish-looking half-breed Jervase Cradock. The tale is very much a pastiche of Machen, much as T.E.D. Klein's *The Ceremonies* is. And like Klein's novel, it is a hugely successful pastiche, one that truly engages the original in the author's own voice and with the author's own concerns. It is both pastiche and original, as much Lovecraft as it is Machen, and it draws strength from both parents. If, as Joshi says, "The Dunwich Horror" made the rest of the Cthulhu Mythos possible, it was only because "they have eyes, but do not see." The resultant pastiches of Lovecraft are far less skilled (for the most part) than HPL's pastiche of Machen. The exceptions—Ramsey Campbell, David Drake, Karl Edward Wagner, Nick Mamatas, Robert Charles Wilson, China Miéville, even Stephen King—are those who respond to Lovecraft on their own terms and in their own voice.

****

So what's up with the moral polarity, then? Lovecraft takes it from Machen, for the most part, although the letter that Joshi cites in the notes is interesting:

I found myself psychologically identifying with one of the characters (an aged scholar who finally combats the menace) toward the end.

Lovecraft wrote this letter, interestingly, to August Derleth—perhaps Derleth had just a trifle more justification for his Manichean Mythos than we like to think? In this mode, Price gleefully notes that the only actual *Necronomicon* quotation (besides Alhazred's couplet) that we have from the master's own hand (from, as it happens, this very story) strongly supports the "Derlethian" concept of a War in Heaven:

> *The ice desert of the South and the sunken isles of Ocean hold stones where Their seal is engraven, but who hath seen the deep frozen city or the sealed tower long garlanded with seaweed and barnacles? Great Cthulhu is Their cousin, yet can he spy Them only dimly.*

If the "sealed tower" is R'lyeh, it implies that Cthulhu, "cousin" though he may be, is sealed in with the seal of the Old Ones, who also destroyed Kadath (most likely the crinoid city in Antarctica, in this context). This is still not very close to the pure Derlethian conception of the benevolent Elder Gods—the "Old Ones" sound, if anything, even worse than Cthulhu and his ilk—but it's far from the conventional wisdom which calls the whole Mythos the naïve deification of abstract or purely alien forces. Of course, one can salvage such a message by reminding the would-be neo-Derlethian that Abdul Alhazred was just such a naïve cultist, foolishly anthropomorphizing the cosmic history of Earth, and that we only see the true version dimly, as through a telescope trained on Sentinel Hill.

****

Once you realize that "The Dunwich Horror" is a Machen pastiche, the next step is to apply it to Machen's concepts of good and evil, not Lovecraft's. And as it happens, we have such a thing explicated, in perhaps the most brilliant philosophical dialogue in all weird fiction, namely the introit to "The White People." Although my favorite bit is Ambrose's famous question:

> *What would your feelings be, seriously, if your cat or your dog began to talk to you, and to dispute with you in human accents? You would be overwhelmed with horror. I am sure of it. And if the roses in your garden sang a weird song, you would go mad. And suppose the stones in the road began to swell and grow before your eyes, and if the pebble that you noticed at night had shot out stony blossoms in the morning?*

The actual answer to the question lies a little further in, when Ambrose says "[sin] is simply an attempt to penetrate into another and higher sphere in a forbidden manner." And there you have the sin of the Whateleys, and the equally necessary response of Armitage. Note that to Lovecraft, there is no forbidden manner of exploration, though some manners are very unwise. But to an exuberant, if eccentric, Christian like Machen, the "forbidden" is very real.

****

So where do we find the Lovecraft in our Machen pastiche? In the structure of the story as, if you will, competing Gospels. Just as "The Shadow Over Innsmouth" is a story of two colliding world-views (a Cargo Cult narrative, as we'll see), "The Dunwich Horror" is a story—almost a holographic interface—of two competing stories. Both the Horror and Armitage are Christ-figures. The Horror is explicitly, almost insultingly, Christological—conceived by an infinite god, born of a virgin on a corner of the year, prodigiously learned at a young age, prophesied over, emerged from a backwater to challenge the priests of the Old Law. Then he dies like Dionysus or Osiris (torn to shreds by wild beasts) and like Christ (on a hilltop calling for his Father)—and like them both, he will be resurrected when the End Times come. ("After summer is winter and after winter summer.") Like Christ, he has two natures, visible and invisible, god and man.

Meanwhile, Armitage is a learned man, a man of (stereotypical) goodness, who rejects the Devil (in a library, pace our previous discussion about libraries as Lovecraftian gardens), who takes on his shoulders the burden of saving the world on a hilltop—the image of three figures on a hill, rejected by those they would save, suffering for all mankind is not comical, regardless of what Joshi claims to think. Armitage is, admittedly, a secular kind of Christ—his purity comes from age, tenure, art (he has a D. Litt.) and learning, not from God or Heaven. But then, he's a Lovecraftian Christ-figure.

****

So why does Good win, then? I think the secret here is in Lovecraft's discovery of identification with Armitage, which I mentioned above. Dunwich represents everything Lovecraft truly fears about society—degeneration. Dunwich begins as a "saving remnant" fled from theocratic Salem, a shining city on Sentinel Hill. Its entire social development occurs during Lovecraft's beloved eighteenth century, but it falls, and its people (again, all whites of good stock) have "gone far along that path of retrogression" back to "almost unnameable violence and perversity." For Lovecraft, degeneration is tied in with a lot of freight—his scientific, Progressive eugenic concerns (the Dunwich folk are Kallikaks, pure and simple), his love of the Edenic Augustan past and his hatred of mongrel modern culture, his discomfort (or at least bafflement) with sex and its associations, his own unfortunate family history of bankruptcy and madness, his actual trips to collapsed and broken New England towns, his fears (financial, social, political) of the future. These fears are clear and present in the Lovecraftian apocalypse of "Nyarlathotep," "He," and especially in "Call of Cthulhu":

> *The time would be easy to know, for then mankind would have become as the Great Old Ones; free and wild and beyond good and evil, with laws and morals thrown aside and all men shouting and killing and revelling in joy.*

This is the future that Lovecraft's mechanist materialism sees coming, inevitably, fatally, and inescapably. All the world will be Dunwich, and Providence will fall.

In Armitage, he created a character with all those same concerns—but with the knowledge and the willpower to reverse them. Armitage is doing what Lovecraft wishes he could, just as Randolph Carter does, and as his other self-identification figures—Jervas Dudley, Charles Dexter Ward—try to. Machen doesn't write tragedy, because Machen believes in redemption. Lovecraft, writing a Machen piece, found that he could believe in redemption from his own philosophy, at least for the length of a story. This poignance, perhaps more than any of the brilliant structure or haunting mood, makes "The Dunwich Horror" succeed. Despite the melodrama.

The Whisperer in Darkness

[February–September 1930]

"The Whisperer in Darkness" is, perhaps, the paradigmatic Cthulhu Mythos story, for good and for ill. Mostly for ill, of course, because people who can't come up with their own ideas wind up regurgitating half-digested versions of this story—man gets odd letter, man goes to creepy New England location, man receives great honking mass of expository material complete with laundry list of weird names, man refuses to act sensibly upon receipt of such information, man idiotically endangers self to advance plot, man is unmanned by terrifying revelation thoroughly foreshadowed in earlier exposition dump, the end—over and over and over and over until, sadly, it becomes very, very difficult to re-read "Whisperer" with a good humor and an open mind. With the best will in the world, I find it hard to forgive Lin Carter for doing his bit to raise it to such prominence as the keynote piece in his anthology *Spawn of Cthulhu*.

****

Which is a real shame, because if you can force yourself to forget about all the smudged copies hacked out over the last 70-odd years, "Whisperer" is a pretty terrific story, combining the "occult detective" structure with the positively Fortean enigma of the Outer Ones, all buttressed by Lovecraft's habitual obsessive emotional and aesthetic verisimilitude for New England terroir:

> *My object* [wrote HPL to Derleth, who obviously didn't get it] *in writing "The Whisperer in Darkness" was not just to be weird, but primarily to crystallize a powerful imaginative impression given me by a certain landscape.*

"Whisperer" is about rationality drowned by too much input, and it can be read as a kind of Heisenbergian updating of the old Newtonian horror universe. In this world, you can't even specifically locate the monsters—are they fungi? lobsters? alive? dead? sorcerers? scientists? ancient? modern? good? evil? Nyarlathotep? winged Indian demons? aliens?—much less find their wolvesbane or garlic and defeat them. Lovecraft takes the shadows and uncertainty and moves them from literary technique to scientific description—the Outer Ones are uncertain and indefinable, no matter how much you know about them. The seemingly clumsy morass of exposition is, again, part of the point. There's too much data, and it absolutely cannot be assembled into a coherent picture. If you doubt any of it, you must doubt all of it—and sure enough, it all vanishes, along with Akeley.

Re-read this alongside John Keel's *The Mothman Prophecies*, not as a "Cthulhu Mythos" story (whatever that means) but as a story of cryptozoology and alien contact and haunting.

AT THE MOUNTAINS OF MADNESS

[FEBRUARY 24-MARCH 22, 1931]

What has haunted my dreams for nearly forty years is a strange sense of adventurous expectancy connected with landscape and architecture and sky-effects.... I wish I could get the idea on paper—the sense of marvel and liberation hiding in obscure dimensions and problematically reachable at rare instances through vistas of ancient streets, across leagues of strange hill country, or up endless flights of marble steps culminating in tiers of balustraded terraces. Odd stuff—and needing a greater poet then I for effective aesthetic utilization...

— H.P. LOVECRAFT, LETTER TO AUGUST DERLETH, JAN. 1930

This quote is true, not only of Lovecraft, but of myself, although my architectural sensibilities are more urban and more modern than his, so I would substitute "vistas of neglected alleys" and "up endless flights of granite and steel setbacks culminating in dizzying chrome and glass coronets" or some such. One can (or at least I can) get "adventurous expectancy" also from hidden literary allusions (*The Crying of Lot 49*), hinted conspiracies, or even sufficiently ill-tended archives. In adventure movies it gives me the sense that the movie is still happening outside the frame, and I occasionally absorb it from such things as the pseudomythology in the background of *Ghostbusters* ("During the rectification of the Vuldronaii, the traveler came as a large and moving Torb! Then, during the third reconciliation of the last of the Mekhetrex supplicants, they chose a new form for him, that of a giant Sloar!") and, of course, from Lovecraft's own para-history. I've attempted it myself throughout **GURPS Cabal**, among other works.

But more importantly, this quote, and this concept, is a vital key for unlocking what Lovecraft was attempting aesthetically, not merely in his Innsmouth and in the haloed Providence of *Charles Dexter Ward*, but in the hills outside Dunwich and the ice deserts of Antarctica. As Joshi points out in a note to this novel (n. 33 in the Penguin edition), Lovecraft uses the term "adventurous expectancy" in Dyer's recounting of the Miskatonic Expedition.

****

This novel (of novella length) is a deliberate attempt at what Robert M. Price calls "demythologization," but which I think is better expressed as "re-mythologization" of the Cthulhu Mythos. It is a hard-core SF story of alien contact, a cutting-edge technothriller at the real-world fringe of scientific exploration, and a punishing, hard-bitten story of psychological disintegration. And again, as with most of Lovecraft's real masterpieces, there's not a lot of useful commentary to add. It's a kind of re-imagining (not a sequel) of Poe's *Arthur Gordon Pym*, with plenty of contributions from Verne and a purely Lovecraftian bleak humor as the humans and Old Ones serially vivisect each other (shades of "Reanimator"!), while only slowly becoming aware of the surviving shoggoths that still hunt both.

****

What do I mean by "remythologization"? I mean a couple of somewhat related things. Before I get to them, let's hear from Lovecraft on the purpose of belief in the scientific age:

It is, then, our task to save existence from a sense of chaos & futility by rebuilding the purely aesthetic & philosophical concept of character & cosmic pseudo-purpose—reestablishing a realisation of the necessity of pattern in any order of being complex enough to satisfy the mind & emotions of highly evolved human personalities.

This passage, from an October 1933 letter to Helen Sully, comes close to providing not just a moral purpose for human action, but perhaps even an artistic purpose for writing about the chaotic and futile cosmos. It's essentially the weird tale as Platonic noble lie. Or, to put it another way, as remythologization.

****

So back to "remythologization" and the two somewhat related meanings, or aims, I give the term, or the project.

First, Lovecraft was attempting to provide a plausible entryway for "adventurous expectancy" not through a world-view that saw everything as magic (or divine) but through a new world-view, one that saw everything as rational. To provide an example of what Lovecraft *did not* want to do: Part of the reason we have "steampunk" in all its variations is that it is easier to get "adventurous expectancy" from the romantic than the familiar[9]. (Cf. Wordsworth's "The World is Too Much With Us.") Lovecraft (and Poe, in *Pym*) didn't take the easy way out and present a romantic past, but a hard-bitten present day of Antarctic exploration. It's obviously much harder to pull that off, although Verne and Wells and company were pointing the way toward such things for a few decades before Lovecraft, presenting the very vastness and immensity of our technological potential, and of the natural world (and cosmos), as subjects of wonder and ter-

---

9. Steampunk is also, it suddenly occurs to me, a kind of domestication of technological unease, analogous to the Victorian domestication of the fairy tale.

ror. Lovecraft's mythology attempts to answer the same questions about the universe, and provide the same cosmic thrills, as all mythologies, but Lovecraft insists—in *At the Mountains of Madness,* at least—that the answers are grounded in geology, and biology, and paleontology, while still scaring the bejezus out of us.

The other sense in which I use the term is to posit that Lovecraft provides a whole new vocabulary for mythologizing things, a whole new regime of gods and monsters in the world of aliens, genetic constructs, and Theosophically vast panoplies of evolution (both physical and social). This is akin to what Leiber calls Lovecraft's "Copernican Revolution" in horror (moving it from the supernatural to the alien, and from the Earthbound to the cosmic), but I'm aiming for something more specific. Lovecraft conjures and super-charges various modern and post-modern mythemes such as the ancient astronauts (although Jason Colavito goes too far when he ascribes the whole complex to HPL in *The Cult of Alien Gods*), the Antarctic secret (from Hollow Earths to Nazi Refuges), scientific discoveries and secret histories that They are hushing up (although the atheist Lovecraft didn't riff on Biblical themes as much as modern mythomania naturally does), cryptids, alien experimentation on humans, and so forth. Further, Lovecraft re-tunes a bunch of previous mythemes from the Frankenstein/Prometheus (genetically constructed shoggoths, which still live on in our nanotechnological nightmare of a "gray goo" apocalypse), to the taboo Mountain (see modern attitudes to Tibet, Sedona, etc.), to the haunted castle (now an archaeological site, viz. *Exorcist* or Indiana Jones), to the cavernous Underworld (from Kadath to Dulce is a short hop). All he needs in *Mountains* is a UFO or two, and the whole skeleton of modern mythology would be on display in one novella. Lovecraft didn't invent our modern mythology, but he is its Hesiod, and *At the Mountains of Madness* is a twentieth-century *Theogony*.

The Shadow Over Innsmouth

[November–December 1931]

I don't think there's a better structural analysis of this story to be had than Robert M. Price's introduction to *The Innsmouth Cycle*. Among other things, Price makes the point that Obed Marsh is the prophet of a Cargo Cult, one which implicitly casts Lovecraft's New England as a primitive backwater. We tend to oversimplify Cargo Cults as the pieces broken off by a clash between "forward-looking" modernity and "backward-looking" primitivism, when in fact, they are the patterns formed by an overlap between two world-views, both of which have firm myths of their origins and of their end states. Lovecraft's story brilliantly inverts the colonialist understanding of the Cargo Cult by demonstrating that the Other (the non-white, the "Kanak," the foreign) is the far more sophisticated myth, one with a better claim both on the past and the future than white Massachusetts Protestant Christianity. All this, of course, thirty years before the mechanism of the Cargo Cult was at all understood in American academia. Of course, Lovecraft likely picked this inversion up from Theosophy, which he had begun reading to get ideas for deep time stories, and which had formulated the same subversive narrative of Britain and India.

I tend to discount various breathless accounts of Lovecraft's immense intellect, because as a partial autodidact myself, I know just how easy an immense intellect is to fake. But this story shows a firm grasp on the principles of anthropology (and sociology, and how life functions in small towns) that one wouldn't have expected from the insular Lovecraft.

Equally importantly and convincingly, Price analyzes the tale as a vision-quest, a coming-of-age ordeal ritual, which I have to say is pretty dead-on.

****

To an extent, this might also be true of Lovecraft, given that the ending of this story has Olmstead, the protagonist, welcoming the kind of miscegenation that is supposedly one of HPL's unbreakable taboos. On the other hand, I think we can also read this as Lovecraft attempting to get into the head of someone who surrenders to the Reality of the Outside, rather than being truly conquered or destroyed by it as most of his protagonists are. Lovecraft can express empathy with Olmstead without sympathy, just as one could write a story told from the perspective of a genteel Rhode Island racist without being one.

****

And let's not get into the rough waters of the pure-blooded Pacific islanders defeating the Deep One-Kanak hybrids with the "Old Ones'" swastika signs. It's probably a coincidence. Although one almost wishes that Norman Spinrad's alternate Adolf Hitler, the SF author of *The Iron Dream*, had written a Cthulhu Mythos story, just for the sheer glandular extremity of it.

****

For me, by the way, this story is Lovecraft's greatest use of setting—and Lovecraft was an absolute master at setting. I drew a map of Innsmouth right after reading this story for the second time, and I can still see the sawgrass in the rusting Rowley spur line if I think about it.

The first time I ever read this story, though, was by the mercury light on the dock at camp, where I had snuck after lights-out and curfew. So I can also still hear the lapping of water on rotten wood, and feel the wet air and mosquitoes, if I try. So that may be why it evokes its setting so very, very well in my mind.

The Dreams in the Witch House

[February 1932]

In his really quite excellent and thorough study *A Subtler Magick: The Writings and Philosophy of H.P. Lovecraft*, Joshi approvingly quotes Stephen J. Mariconda's description of this tale as "Lovecraft's magnificent failure."

Well, he's half right. The story is magnificent. It is only a failure insofar as it doesn't complete a full Lovecraftian arc. One of Joshi's sounder arguments (possibly adapted from George Wetzel?) is that Lovecraft had only a very limited repertoire of story-elements, and that he continuously reused them, refining them as he went until eventually they became true masterpieces. So you can pick apart the earliest tales—such as "Dagon," "The Tomb," and "Polaris"—and discover the skeletons, if you will, of "Call of Cthulhu" (primordial sea cult alive in nightmares), *Charles Dexter Ward* (antiquarian shares soul with evil ancestor), and "The Shadow Out of Time" (man switches consciousness between aeons to the detriment of his identity). Obviously, some of—most of—the later masterworks draw skeletal elements from more than one early source, and some of the early elements are never really developed later (as with about half of the material in "The Tomb"), but the general progression is, I think, fairly clear.

I would argue that "The Dreams in the Witch House" is the almost-completed version of the skeleton first laid down in "From Beyond," (man perceives Outside, Outside comes in) and that (with "Call of Cthulhu") it is actually one of the purest and most important examples of sheer Lovecraftian cosmicism. (Other major iterations of the "From Beyond story" include "The Music of Erich Zann," "Hypnos," "The Hound," "He," and "Strange High House in the Mist"—although you could easily discover the "From Beyond story" in "Pickman's Model,"

"The Dunwich Horror" (in negative form), and "The Haunter of the Dark" among others.) What it *isn't* is a fully perfected version of this story—it's not "Call of Cthulhu" or *Charles Dexter Ward*, in other words. There's at least one more iteration of this fugue left in Lovecraft, and unless you consider "Haunter of the Dark" to be the missing apotheosis, HPL never got around to writing it.

So it's not Lovecraft's best story by any means. (I'd call it about his tenth-best story.) But it is absolutely not a failure, and not at all the "step backward in his fictional development" (whatever that nonsensical phrase means, applied to a Lovecraft story written after 1925) that Joshi insinuates. Joshi, I think, really, really hates the crucifix, the Black Man, the trappings of witchcraft and evil and black magic in what (to him) should be a stark blast of cosmic higher mathematics. In fact, in *A Subtler Magick*, Joshi gives us his specific complaints, which (aside from defensibly, if exaggeratedly, objecting to the prose style of the story—Gilman is something of a Poe-character, and there are indeed a few lapses) uniformly circle around this 'historicizing' material. Joshi's objections are almost cartoonishly facile, and my answers are similarly impatient:

"What is the significance of the Old Ones in the story?"

They indicate that hyperspace travel goes through time as well as space, and otherwise perform the same function that all of Lovecraft's Mythos callbacks perform, enhancing cosmicism.

"To what purpose is the baby kidnapped and sacrificed?"

We don't know. It's a purposeless horror, on purpose. Gilman is meant to be off-balance the whole time, and Joshi can't possibly believe the story would be better if Gilman, Keziah Mason, and Brown Jenkin got together on Walpurgisnacht and did *really hard math!* Any roleplaying game player can come up with a million possible reasons that Keziah would carry out such sacrifices, and any horror or SF fan—or even a critic who writes long divagatory books on the weird tale—should be able to stump up one or two good ones.

"How can Lovecraft the atheist allow Keziah to be frightened off by the sight of a crucifix?"

Hmmm. Let's see. Maybe characters aren't their authors? Maybe Keziah Mason, a 17th century witch and initiate of a witch-cult persecuted (for good reason) by cross-wielding folks, might be frightened briefly—not "off" as Joshi mischaracterizes the event—by a crucifix? Maybe in faultless Freudian fashion her subconscious is still anti-Christian instead of cosmically atheist? Either way, Joshi misses the joke, that Gilman winds up strangling Keziah with the chain of the crucifix—it has no magic witch-repelling power.

"Why does Nyarlathotep appear in the conventional figure of the Black Man?"

For the same reason that he appears that way in both the sonnet and prose-poem that bear his name? And maybe because he was summoned by a 17th-century European witch in the form that she expected—that she calculated, if you will—instead of as the Large And Moving Sloar?

"In the final confrontation with Keziah, what is the purpose of the abyss aside from providing a convenient place down which to kick Brown Jenkin?"

Well, Joshi's got me there. In all my time spent in hyperspatial witch-attics, I've never seen an abyss, and Lovecraft is being downright unrealistic... Seriously, what kind of asinine question is this?

"How does Brown Jenkin subsequently emerge from the abyss to eat out Gilman's heart?"

Didn't Joshi just complain that we don't know what the abyss does? Does he even read his own chapters? Maybe it's a wormhole. Maybe Brown Jenkin—being the one who taught Keziah to use hyperspace, after all—is really good at emerging from abysses.

Hey, but don't worry, S.T.—August Derleth didn't much like this story either.

THROUGH THE GATES
OF THE SILVER KEY

[PRICE: AUGUST 1932; HPL: OCTOBER? 1932-APRIL 1933]

I will say this—this is some kinda slam-bang story. There's more wonderful loose ends, trippy metaphysics, and crazy fizzy-pop ideas in this story than in virtually any other Lovecraft tale of like length. And at the end, nothing much has happened—Carter is still missing, the time is still (literally) out of joint, and all we've got is tapir prints in the carpet and the comforting knowledge that in the year 2169 Pickman Carter will kick "the Mongol hordes" out of Australia.

****

This is the only multiple-author story that Joshi sees fit to include in the Penguin series. On the one hand, this is defensible on the grounds that it concludes the "Randolph Carter Cycle" of tales. On the other, it definitely suffers by comparison to the pure-quill Lovecraft surrounding it.

This is not an inevitable outcome of Lovecraft's collaborations. Counting his ghost-writing and revision work as "collaboration," some of it was quite successful. I think "The Mound," "The Curse of Yig," and "Out of the Aeons" are worthy components of the canon at all but the highest levels—certainly they bear comparison to, say, "The Shunned House" or even "Haunter of the Dark."

On a lower level—say "Picture in the House" or so—"The Last Test" and "Medusa's Coil" are surprisingly effective on a lot of levels, too, and I enjoy the over-the-top qualities of "The Horror in the Museum." "The Challenge From Beyond" is fun for what it is, namely an exquisite corpse.

A lot of people praise "The Night Ocean" very highly, but I'm not sure I've read it recently (or closely) enough to know what they're talking about. I don't remember being blown away by it, though.

That said, in contrarian fashion I'm quite fond of "The Horror at Martin's Beach," which HPL co-wrote with his wife Sonia, but then I'm just a big romantic who loves sea serpents.

****

Theosophists have guessed at the awesome grandeur of the cosmic cycle wherein our world and human race form transient incidents. They have hinted at strange survivals in terms which would freeze the blood if not masked by a bland optimism.

— H.P. Lovecraft, "The Call of Cthulhu"

Given that "Through the Gates of the Silver Key" combines Orientalism, time-travel, cyclical metaphysics, alien races, and malarkey, it's as good a place as any to pause and discuss Theosophy and Lovecraft. Without going into mind-numbing detail, Theosophy was an attempt to extrapolate Darwinian science and Hindu mysticism into a single belief system. Its central teachings, as set forth in *Isis Unveiled* (1877) and *The Secret Doctrine* (1888), and as horribly simplified by me, held that over immense periods of time—millions and billions of years—numerous sentient races arose, flourished, advanced, and fell on the Earth in cycles punctuated by continental-scale cataclysms. These races were slowly degenerating from pure spirit into pure matter: our human race, the Fifth, is the lamest of the bunch so far. (Each race has a Root Race; ours is the "Aryan." Mmm-hmmm.) It achieved a certain vogue around the turn of the 20th century, and its creator Helena P. Blavatsky (often referred to as "HPB" in fine parallel with our own "HPL") managed to have rather more influence on a certain stratum of intellect than your standard former carnival trick-rider normally does. Even now, post-Blavatskyan Theosophy remains a core component of the New Age and neo-paganism generally, and in Lovecraft's time, the heyday of such superficially similar cosmic historian-poets as Oswald Spengler and Olaf Stapledon, it absolutely ruled the occult roost.

By 1925/1926—precisely the time he was plotting and writing "The Call of Cthulhu"—Lovecraft discovered Theosophy, through a compilation (*Atlantis and Lost Lemuria*) by one of its later proselytes, W. Scott-Elliot. In June of 1926, he is writing to Clark Ashton Smith:

> *Really, some of these hints about the lost 'City of the Golden Gates' & the shapeless monsters of ancient Lemuria are ineffably pregnant with fantastic suggestion; & I only wish I could get hold of more of the stuff.*

His hookup for "the stuff" seems to have been E. Hoffmann Price, his collaborator on "Through the Gates of the Silver Key," and (as far as I can tell with admittedly minimal research) not a Theosophist himself. Price was a pulp writer, a friend of *Weird Tales* editor Farnsworth Wright, and a correspondent of Robert E. Howard. Howard arranged for Price and Lovecraft to meet during HPL's June 1932 visit to New Orleans. The two hit it off, and Price gave Lovecraft either a précis or copious notes on "the Pushkara-Plaksha-Kusha-Shâlmali-Mt. Wern-Senzar-Dzyan-Shamballah myth-cycle" in early 1933, likely to encourage work on this story. Again (in a February 18, 1933 letter), Lovecraft tips off Smith: "I don't know where E. Hoffmann got hold of this stuff, but it sounds damn good." By 1936, he is lecturing his other correspondents on the topic, writing on June 19 to Frederic Jay Pabody:

> *One may add that these European myths [of Atlantis] have nothing to do with the early Hindoo myths on which the theosophists draw. The identification of the lost world Kusha with 'Atlantis' was a mere gesture of the 19th century mystagogues.*

Lovecraft noticed the commonalities between Theosophy, with its primordial inhuman species following divergent physical laws while remaining subject to the inevitable grindings of evolution and entropy, and the para-paleontology he was developing. As he wrote to Elizabeth Toldridge in March of 1933:

> *All this sounds amusingly like the synthetic mythology I have concocted for my stories, but Price assures me it is actual folklore & promises to send further particulars.*

Price may have been over-egging the pudding a bit calling the sheerly chimerical Theosophy "actual folklore," or he may have been taken in by one of the many domestic Indian or Tamil mythomanes that took Theosophy as their base, often for political purposes.

Blavatsky's (fabricated) "*Book of Dzyan*" made it, via Price, into the pile of moldering Mythos tomes Robert Blake discovers in "The Haunter of the Dark." It played an even bigger role (along with Shamballah) in Lovecraft's revision tale "The Diary of Alonzo Typer," and the quasi-Theosophical Mu appears in the revision "Out of the Aeons." "The Children of the Fire Mist" in "Through the Gates of the Silver Key" are likewise Theosophical angel-figures, who (pace Scott-Elliot) descended to Earth from Venus.

The Great Race of Yith in "Shadow Out of Time," for example, has no physical form, existing only as mentation; the close parallel to the purely psychic Polarians, the "First Root Race" of Theosophy, is remarkable, and intentional. Lovecraft gives us the nod in that tale: "A few of the myths had significant connections with other cloudy legends of the prehuman world, especially those Hindu tales involving stupefying gulfs of time and forming part of the lore of modern theosophists."

Other specific influences are a little iffier. In his essay "HPL and HPB" (from which I have gladly lifted much of this information), Robert M. Price postulates that Lovecraft's "Cyclopean" architecture derives from Theosophical giant-lore (the Lemurians and Atlanteans, Root Races Three and Four, were both gigantic). He also speculates that "the undying leaders" of the Cthulhu cult "in the mountains of China" (mentioned in "The Call of Cthulhu") are a reference to the Ascended Masters of Theosophy, who dwell in Tibet, which is surely close enough. I don't buy the first—Lovecraft's use of "Cyclopean" goes back to "Dagon"—but the second seems more than plausible, given the number of shout-outs to Theosophy in "Call of Cthulhu," and the fact that Lovecraft seems to have discovered Theosophy practically in the midst of plotting the tale.

THE THING ON THE DOORSTEP

[August 21-24, 1933]

When Lin Carter doesn't like a Lovecraft story, I think the critical battle for acceptance is officially over. "The Thing on the Doorstep" is universally acknowledged to be a disappointment, or even an outright failure. (Even by HPL, who eventually allowed Julius Schwartz to badger him into submitting it three years after it was written.) I know that it's one of the few HPL stories I've never bothered to re-read (until now), and although I occasionally enjoying putting my thumb in the critical eye, I have to agree that it's definitely lesser Lovecraft.

That said, the character of the unfortunate Edward Pickman Derby is actually fairly acutely drawn and interesting, and (like his vague model Charles Dexter Ward) his personality actually moves the plot rather than being convenient to it, unlike so many Lovecraft protagonists. For that alone, I think the story repays some study, although obviously there are hordes of other writers to turn to for competent character-driven fiction. Only Lovecraft can deliver us our cosmic smack, and here he steps on it way too much.

****

With that said, in the Lovecraftian universe, there would logically be such minor domestic tragedies as this. Yet more lives deformed and shoved askew by the passage of cosmic forces—forces, in this case, completely unaware of how human sorcerers are tugging at their shoelaces and pretending to control them. The sense of human sorcery as Cargo Cult, picking up barely-understood bits and techniques of an unthinkably advanced species' physics, could come through quite well in a story like this, and glimmers yet beneath this one if you let it.

****

I do disagree with Cannon and Joshi, when they accuse the Arkham background of "Doorstep" of being sketched in. As opposed to most of the Lovecraft canon, Arkham begins to come alive as a place where people do things besides read crumbling tomes in the library. It's still fairly thin mead—we know far, far more about Innsmouth or Dunwich, which we only visit in one tale apiece, than we ever learn about the supposed center of Lovecraft's fictional "Miskatonic Country." But I like the hints of Arkham society and stratification Lovecraft adds, mostly in desperate attempts to conceal how truly unfitted he is to write anything like this story.

****

One does wonder what Sonia Greene's reaction to reading this story in *Weird Tales* might have been. She doesn't mention it in her memoir of HPL, and of course it wasn't published until a decade after the failure of their marriage, but still. One doesn't have to be Sigmund Freud, or even S.T. Joshi, to read some of Lovecraft's reaction to married life into the psychic imprisonment of Derby by Asenath.

****

George Wetzel adduces this tale to Lovecraft's "common soul" (or "psychic possession") trope, along with "The Tomb," "The Shadow Out of Time," *Charles Dexter Ward* (controversially, but I think the theme is clear even if the crux of the actual story is about physical, not psychic, replacement), "The Challenge From Beyond," "Wall of Sleep," and (intriguingly) "The Festival," "Colour Out of Space," and "Haunter of the Dark." I would add, perhaps at one remove, "The Call of Cthulhu," (which is, after all, about Cthulhu's dream-soul deforming those it encounters) and perhaps even "The Shadow Over Innsmouth," which is certainly about the replacement of a human soul by that of a Deep One, possibly triggered by physical change or trauma, or possibly merely by exposure, as in "Colour." I also recall the slow melding of perspectives and insights between man and crinoid in *At the Mountains of Madness*.

Learning the alien truth makes us alien… Is there a connection here to Derby's wild accusations that shoggoths are somehow involved in Waite's sorcery? What is a shoggoth, after all, but the common soul at its most basic, even quantum form, able to take any form and none, fully plastic and completely undefined?

So all in all, it's a damn shame that the story's not that good, isn't it?

THE SHADOW OUT OF TIME

[FALL 1934 TO FEBRUARY 22, 1935]

In many ways the story is the culmination of Lovecraft's fictional career, and by no means an unfitting capstone to a twenty-year attempt to capture the sense of wonder and awe felt at the boundless reaches of space and time.
— S.T. JOSHI, INTRODUCTION TO
THE SHADOW OUT OF TIME: THE CORRECTED TEXT

[Lovecraft's] single greatest achievement in fiction. The form and substance of this extraordinary novella, its amazing scope and sense of cosmic immensitude, the gulfs of time it opens, the titanic sweep of the narrative… one of the most tremendously exciting imaginative experiences I have yet found in fantastic fiction …
— LIN CARTER, LOVECRAFT: A LOOK BEHIND THE CTHULHU MYTHOS

By the way—I finished 'Shadow Out of Time' last week, but doubt whether it is good enough to type. Somehow or other, it does not seem to embody quite what I want to embody—and I may tear it up and start all over again.
— H.P. LOVECRAFT,
LETTER TO E. HOFFMANN PRICE, MARCH 14, 1935

Of the three of them, I tend more toward Lovecraft's opinion of "Shadow Out of Time," although it's far and away good enough to type. It's merely great, though, not transcendent. I think I lowball it for some ill-defined reason, one that Lovecraft put best—for me, too, it does not seem to embody quite what it could. It's more than a little over-long, and I find very little suspense to the final denouement. Well, technically, none whatsoever. It's a surgically neat climax, but that's the best I can say of it. Maybe if we really got into Peaslee's head, we could feel his shock more fully, but overtypically, Peaslee is a boring stick who spends more time than Lovecraft can believably convey in agonies of Poe-narrative indecision about his experience. Even Australia (with its huge potential for the outré) isn't really milked and brought to unlife the way Lovecraft does Antarctica in *At the Mountains of Madness*. My "adventurous expectancy" is sated early, when Peaslee susses out the core myth of Pnakotic possession, and I never really get it back.

I also wonder how you keep your identical handwriting if your mind is immured in a seven-foot-tall cone-being. This isn't just nitpicking. I am somewhat surprised that Joshi doesn't see (and on past form, stridently object to) the hugely obvious negation of "mechanist materialism" in the assumption that mentation and personality (even memory, in Peaslee's case)—the soul, in other words—is independent of the physical brain, or even of humanoid brain structure. (In Lovecraft's original version of this tale, the mind-transfers were from ancient—but human—Lomar.)

I do love the cosmicism; the stark vastness of time, the great allusion to Buddai ("the gigantic old man who lies asleep for ages underground with his head on his arm, and who will some day awake and eat up the world"), the increasingly deft retournement of the *Necronomicon* (this time as 'dream diary'), and what we see of Peaslee's attempt to discover his bizarre activities while "amnesiac." I especially love the horrible, horrible Yithians with their "fascistic socialism," their callous voyeurism, and their utter amorality bred of utter invulnerability. ("Flying polyps going to escape, eh?" "Not our problem. It's off to beetle-time we go." BAMF.) Lovecraft never blended the alien and the villainous as convincingly.

But I just don't love this story as I probably should.

THE HAUNTER OF THE DARK

[NOVEMBER 5-9, 1935]

To set us up for Lovecraft's last story, a quote from Lovecraft's last letter:

There is no drawing a line betwixt what is to be called extreme fantasy of a traditional type and what is to be called surrealism; and I have no doubt but that the nightmare landscapes of some of the surrealists correspond, as well as any actual creations could, to the iconographic horrors attributed by sundry fictioneers to mad or daemon-haunted artists. If there were a real Richard Upton Pickman…I am sure he would have been represented in the recent exhibition by several blasphemous and abhorrent canvases!

Robert Blake, in addition to being a manque for Robert Bloch, is a painter, and this may partially explain Lovecraft's Expressionist, almost surrealistic, approach to this story. (Part of it is also no doubt that he dashed it off in four days as a kind of inside joke.)

For example, the normally exquisitely meticulous Lovecraft shows a shocking lack of concern about the effects of light on the Haunter—a little light (filtered through the steeple windows into the open box) keeps the Haunter at bay, but Blake writes "of the duty of burying the Shining Trapezohedron and of banishing what he had evoked by letting daylight into the hideous spire." To the contrary, Blake apparently summons the thing by closing the box and thus cutting the Trapezohedron (both "Shining" and the source of an ultimate fuligin darkness) off from the light. At the end, lightning banishes the Haunter, but the good "Dr. Dexter" buries the box in constant darkness, in "the deepest channel of Narragansett Bay." This is consistent with the Trapezohedron's history—it's inactive while underwater—but not with Blake's experience. (Bloch had fun with this inconsistency in his own sequel to the story, "The Shadow From the Steeple.")

Elsewhere, there's the tendency of the Trapezohedron to move around the church at random; the ridiculous amount of time and effort Blake takes to walk two miles across town (even while dying of cancer, HPL rambled for miles at a time on a whim); the intrepid and surprisingly chatty (or at least informative) skeleton; the Cook's Tour of Ancient Times; the beautiful Gothic ending complete with Poe reference, blackout, and lightning-storm (although Lovecraft's instinctual verisimilitude forced him—or allowed him—to use a real, historical thunderstorm); and the surfeit of magical texts just lying around in the Starry Wisdom church. ("He wondered how they could have remained undisturbed for so long." No kidding.) Not the language (which is relatively restrained even for late Lovecraft) but the incidents of the story are highly colored, exaggerated for effect. And as Lovecraft reminds us, this is the "artist's version" of the story. The 'real' facts implicate hoaxing and hysteria.

****

And since the story is actually a jape—HPL killing off his friend Robert Bloch in "revenge" for Bloch doing the same to HPL in his own story "The Shambler From the Stars"—this 'hoax' narrative may be Lovecraft's meta-commentary on his own Mythos, which after all has managed to hoax a lot of people into believing that thre are actual *Necronomicon*s lying around abandoned in Rhode Island churches.

The unreliable narrator "adrift" from his normal course, the dreamlike landscape, the Monster From the Temple, the allusions to antiquity, even the doom at the window and the panicked written climax strongly echo "Dagon," Lovecraft's first *Weird Tales* story, just as the theme of cross-temporal possession and the cleansing lightning bolt echo "The Tomb," his first adult tale.

****

I will briefly interrupt the flow of this thought, such as it is, to express my irritation at being misled by Anton LaVey. LaVey founded the "Order of the Trapezoid," which he borrowed from Lovecraft's "Shining Trapezohedron." Well, turns out that a trapezohedron has nothing to do with trapezoids at all. A trapezohedron is a solid whose faces are kite-shaped quadrilaterals, like a 10-sided die. What I (and apparently LaVey) thought was a trapezohedron—a polyhedron with trapezoids for sides—is actually a frustum. So the Hancock Building, which so delightfully crouches on LaVey's birthplace, is not, despite what I've said in person and print for the better part of 20 years now, the world's largest trapezohedron. It's the world's four largest trapezoids, leaned up to make a frustum. Stupid Satanists, wrecking it for everybody.

****

But math-crazy Lovecraft would have known that a trapezohedron is an "antiprism." Something, in other words, that sucks up all colors and melds them into darkness.

****

At any rate, the story also, as I re-read it for this exercise, seemed to hint at another set of echoes, although I can't quite explain them. This, then, is not even the kind of tossed-off literary criticism I've engaged in above; it's completely unjustified, *Suppressed-Transmission*-level silliness.

But…isn't the Trapezohedron an awful lot like the Grail? It's found in a Perilous Chapel, which seems to exist in an Otherworld ("he half fancied that the Federal Hill of that distant view was a dream-world never to be trod by living human feet"), by a young and inexperienced quester who doesn't even know what he's looking for. (Not to beat this to death, but "Edmund Fiske," the Fritz Leiber manque from Bloch's sequel, has a sort of Gawain-esque irascibility to him, just as "Blake" has a Percival-like simplicity. There don't seem to be any Galahads in the Mythos.) The Grail vouchsafes visions, specifically processions and hallows, to the quester. (In addition to "processions of robed, hooded figures," Blake has a vision of Azathoth—the inverse of the Grail's vision of God.)

The Grail is tied to some sort of god-king (Haunter/Nyarlathotep), who when the quester finds him, is faint and feeble. (For more Jessie Westonosity, Blake arrives in the winter, enters the church in spring—"late in April"—and the Haunter emerges at full strength in high summer.) The quester gains wisdom from an old man (either Lillibridge's skeleton, or perhaps even the Lovecraft-manque from Bloch's "Shambler") and returns to the Castle able to answer the questions (after learning the Trapezohedron's history, Blake sleepwalks back to the church and dreams the truth) and achieves the Grail, being adopted into its lineage and taken into the Otherworld (Blake joins minds with the Haunter and dies); the Grail is taken up into Heaven (dropped into the deepest channel of the Sea, a clear anti-Ascension). Like I say, I have no evidence that this is what Lovecraft means—he doesn't seem to have owned a copy of Jessie Weston's pioneering Grail study *From Ritual to Romance*, I haven't turned up any evidence that he ever bothered much with Grail lore, and his letters make plain his belief that Arthur was a Britanno-Roman cataphract—but it's suggestive, as we say in the dark hintings biz.

Conclusion

So we've finished the Tour de Lovecraft, hopefully in better shape than we started it. As a final thought, I'd say this. Lovecraft combined an epochal imagination with a nearly nihilist philosophy—the two ingredients that together make "cosmic horror." But more importantly, Lovecraft was a great writer. Of his solo adult works, 17 of 50 are great by almost any standard. (That's a career .340 average—home run average, that is. And six of those were knocked clean out of the park.) By the time his style fully matured in the mid-1920s, he was almost incapable of turning out a truly bad story. He was a complex writer, who believed (correctly) that both verisimilitude and gothicism depended on intricate structures of both plot and language. A dedicated Anglophone craftsman, HPL is not for the lazy, any more than Faulkner or Borges—or Hawthorne, his great unsung model—are. In his mature phase, he almost never wastes a word: if you can't figure out why it's there, that's your problem, not his. Not all of the mature stories work for all readers—"The Thing on the Doorstep" is probably the weakest of them, and as I've intimated before, "The Silver Key" is perhaps best seen as mental attic-cleaning rather than as fiction in the technical sense. But even those two (clearly his weakest post-1925 tales) are structurally sound as drums, and make interesting reading to boot, two desiderata at which far too many short stories fail.

For all those who say that Lovecraft is all style (and bad style at that) and no substance, why is it that there are no successful pastiches of Lovecraft in his own style? Why aren't we drowning in stories at least as good as "The Shadow Out of Time" or "The Haunter of the Dark"? Why, if it's just a matter of piling up "eldritch unnameables," can't any journeyman hack with Robert M. Price's email address manage it? Why can't even very good craftsmen indeed do it? (August Derleth is no slouch on his own turf, and Robert Bloch and Ramsey Campbell, well, the defense rests.) Why, for that matter, are some of Lovecraft's stories better than others if all it takes to write like Lovecraft is a thesaurus and a lobster-shack menu? No, in the great works there's definitely something there, some "adventurous expectancy," some outside shape scratching "at the known universe's utmost rim."

For all his undoubted skill, knowledge, and perception, I disagree with S.T. Joshi, who sees Lovecraft's art (and by extension all art?) as ancillary to, or derivative upon, the author's philosophy. I disagree with Colin Wilson, who sees Lovecraft's art (and by extension all art?) as ancillary to, or derivative upon, the author's personality, his "sickness," if you will. I disagree with attempts to understand Lovecraft's art as murkily sublimated autobiography. Obviously Lovecraft's beliefs, his mind, and his unhappy life played their role, just like any artist's do. But 1920s New England was full of autodidactic Nietzsche wannabes, many of them also neurasthenic, over-coddled, and bankrupt. It only produced one H.P. Lovecraft.

So I hold that Lovecraft's art—like all great art—is fundamentally of its own origin. It comes from where it comes, be it genius, or the Muses, or the Gates of Deeper Slumber. As HPL wrote to E. Hoffmann Price in 1934: "Art is not what one resolves to say, but what insists on saying itself through one." Lovecraft, like all artists, learned to transmit it, to shape it and tame it for our view, as best he could. The proof is in the pudding: Cthulhu (and all that he stands for) has become as Superman, or Sherlock Holmes, or Robinson Crusoe, or Hamlet, or Lancelot, or Jason and the Argonauts—a timeless icon, a myth. Like all myths it can be endlessly interpreted, set on new pedestals or loudly flung away. Without HPL's craft—and yes, without his "mechanist materialism" and his psychosomatic fish allergies—he could not have revealed Cthulhu to us in just that form. And without his blindness and his lyre Homer couldn't have sung the words he did, either. But now, Troy burns eternally. And *Cthulhu fhtagn.*

SOURCES AND RESOURCES

THE SACRED TEXTS

Lovecraft, H.P., *The Call of Cthulhu and Other Weird Stories,* edited with an introduction and notes by S.T. Joshi (Penguin Books, 1999).

Lovecraft, H.P., *The Thing on the Doorstep and Other Weird Stories,* edited with an introduction and notes by S.T. Joshi (Penguin Books, 2001).

Lovecraft, H.P., *The Dreams in the Witch House and Other Weird Stories,* edited with an introduction and notes by S.T. Joshi (Penguin Books, 2004).

THE COMMENTARIES

Buhle, Paul, "Dystopia as Utopia: Howard Phillips Lovecraft and the Unknown Content of American Horror Literature" [1976], in S.T. Joshi (ed.), *H.P. Lovecraft: Four Decades of Criticism* (Ohio University Press, 1980).

Burke, Edmund, *A Philosophical Enquiry Into the Origin of Our Ideas on the Sublime and Beautiful* [1757], edited by Adam Philips (Oxford University Press, 1998).

Cannon, Peter, "HPL: Problems in Critical Recognition" [1990], in James Van Hise, *The Fantastic Worlds of H.P. Lovecraft* (privately published, 1999).

Cannon, Peter, "The Influence of *Vathek* on H. P. Lovecraft's *The Dream-Quest of Unknown Kadath,*" in S.T. Joshi (ed.), *H.P. Lovecraft: Four Decades of Criticism* (Ohio University Press, 1980).

Cannon, Peter, "Sunset Terrace Imagery in Lovecraft," *Lovecraft Studies* No. 5 (Fall 1981).

Carroll, Noël, *The Philosophy of Horror: or, Paradoxes of the Heart* (Routledge, 1990).

Carter, Lin, *Lovecraft: A Look Behind the "Cthulhu Mythos"* (Ballantine Books, 1972).

Carter, Lin (ed.), *The Spawn of Cthulhu* (Ballantine Books, 1971).

Cavallaro, Dani, *The Gothic Vision: Three Centuries of Horror, Terror and Fear* (Continuum, 2002).

Colavito, Jason, *The Cult of Alien Gods: H.P. Lovecraft and Extraterrestrial Pop Culture* (Prometheus Books, 2005).

Conover, Willis, *Lovecraft at Last* (Carrollton • Clark, 1975).

Davenport-Hines, Richard, *Gothic: Four Hundred Years of Excess, Horror, Evil, and Ruin* (Fourth Estate, 1998).

Davis, Erik, "Calling Cthulhu: H.P. Lovecraft's Magick Realism," in Richard Metzger (ed.), *The Book of Lies: The Disinformation Guide to Magick and the Occult* (Disinformation Company, 2003).

DeCamp, L. Sprague, *Lovecraft: A Biography* (Doubleday, 1975).

Dziemianowicz, Stefan, "Outsiders and Aliens: The Uses of Isolation in Lovecraft's Fiction," in S.T. Joshi and David E. Schultz (eds.), *An Epicure in the Terrible: A Centennial Anthology of Essays in Honor of H.P. Lovecraft* (Fairleigh Dickinson University Press, 1991).

Frierson, Meade and Penny (eds.), *HPL* (privately published, 1972).

Frye, Northrop, *An Anatomy of Criticism: Four Essays* (Princeton University Press, 1957).

Frye, Northrop, *The Secular Scripture: A Study of the Structure of Romance* (Harvard University Press, 1976).

Godwin, Joscelyn, *Arktos: The Polar Myth in Science, Symbolism, and Nazi Survival* (Phanes Press, 1991).

Hite, Kenneth, *Dubious Shards* (Ronin Arts, 2006).

Hoffman, Daniel, *Poe Poe Poe Poe Poe Poe Poe* (Avon Books, 1972).

Houellebecq, Michel, *H.P. Lovecraft: Against the World, Against Life* [1991], translated by Dorna Khazeni (Believer Books, 2005).

Joshi, S.T. (ed.), *The Annotated H.P. Lovecraft* (Dell Publishing, 1997).

Joshi, S.T., "A Chronology of Selected Works by H.P. Lovecraft," in S.T. Joshi (ed.), *H.P. Lovecraft: Four Decades of Criticism* (Ohio University Press, 1980).

Joshi, S.T., and Schultz, David E. (eds.), *An Epicure in the Terrible: A Centennial Anthology of Essays in Honor of H.P. Lovecraft* (Fairleigh Dickinson University Press, 1991).

Joshi, S.T., *H.P. Lovecraft: A Life* (Necronomicon Press, 1996).

Joshi, S.T. (ed.), *H.P. Lovecraft: Four Decades of Criticism* (Ohio University Press, 1980).

Joshi, S.T., *An Index to the Fiction and Poetry of H.P. Lovecraft* (Necronomicon Press, 1992).

Joshi, S.T., *An Index to the Selected Letters of H.P. Lovecraft* (Necronomicon Press, 1980).

Joshi, S.T., *Lovecraft's Library: A Catalogue* (rev. ed., Hippocampus Books, 2002).

Joshi, S.T., and Cannon, Peter (eds.), *More Annotated H.P. Lovecraft* (Dell Publishing, 1999).

Joshi, S.T., *A Subtler Magick: The Writings and Philosophy of H.P. Lovecraft* (Wildside Press, 1999).

Joshi, S.T., *The Weird Tale* (University of Texas Press, 1990).

King, Stephen, *Danse Macabre* (Everest House, 1981).

Leiber, Fritz, "A Literary Copernicus" [1949], in S.T. Joshi (ed.), *H.P. Lovecraft: Four Decades of Criticism* (Ohio University Press, 1980).

Lovecraft, H.P., *Collected Essays, Volume 2: Literary Criticism,* edited by S.T. Joshi (Hippocampus Press, 2004).

Lovecraft, H.P., *Selected Letters, Vols. 1-5,* edited by August Derleth, Donald Wandrei, and James Turner (Arkham House, 1965-1976).

Lovecraft, H.P., *Supernatural Horror in Literature* [1936], edited and annotated by S.T. Joshi (Hippocampus Books, 2000).

Miéville, China, "Introduction," in H.P. Lovecraft, *At the Mountains of Madness: The Definitive Edition* (Modern Library, 2005).

Mosig, Dirk W., "The Four Faces of 'The Outsider'" [1974], in Darrell Schweitzer (ed.), *Discovering H.P. Lovecraft* (Starmont House, 1987).

Mosig, Dirk W., "H.P. Lovecraft: Myth-Maker" [1976], in S.T. Joshi (ed.), *H.P. Lovecraft: Four Decades of Criticism* (Ohio University Press, 1980).

Mosig, Dirk W., *Mosig at Last: A Psychologist Looks at H.P. Lovecraft* (Necronomicon Press, 1997).

Nelson, Victoria, "H.P. Lovecraft and the Great Heresies," in Victoria Nelson, *The Secret Life of Puppets* (Harvard University Press, 2001).

Oates, Joyce Carol, "The King of Weird," *New York Review of Books*, Vol. 43, No. 17 (October 31, 1996).

Oates, Joyce Carol, "Introduction," in Joyce Carol Oates (ed.), *Tales of H.P. Lovecraft* (Ecco, 1997).

Price, Robert M. (ed.), *The Horror of It All: Encrusted Gems From the "Crypt of Cthulhu"* (Starmont House, 1990).

Price, Robert M., "HPL and HPB: Lovecraft's Use of Theosophy" *Crypt of Cthulhu* No. 5 (Roodmas, 1982).

Price, Robert M., "Introduction: Lovecraft's Cosmic History," in Robert M. Price (ed.), *The Antarktos Cycle* (Chaosium, 1999).

Price, Robert M., "Introduction: Ontogeny Recapitulates Phylogeny," in Robert M. Price (ed.), *The Innsmouth Cycle* (Chaosium, 1998).

Price, Robert M., "Introduction: The Other Name of Azathoth," in Robert M. Price (ed.), *The Cthulhu Cycle* (Chaosium, 1996).

Price, Robert M., "Introduction: What Roodmas Horror," in Robert M. Price (ed.), *The Dunwich Cycle* (Chaosium, 1995).

Price, Robert M., "Lovecraft's 'Artificial Mythology'" [1991], in S.T. Joshi and David E. Schultz (eds.), *An Epicure in the Terrible: A Centennial Anthology of Essays in Honor of H.P. Lovecraft* (Fairleigh Dickinson University Press, 1991).

Rateliff, John D., "Classics of Fantasy: *The Dream-Quest of Unknown Kadath* by H.P. Lovecraft," on the Wizards of the Coast website: <http://ww2.wizards.com/books/Wizards/default.aspx?doc=main_classicsdreamquest>

St.-Armand, Barton L., "Facts in the Case of H.P. Lovecraft" [1972], in S.T. Joshi (ed.), *H.P. Lovecraft: Four Decades of Criticism* (Ohio University Press, 1980).

St.-Armand, Barton L., *The Roots of Horror in the Fiction of H.P. Lovecraft* (Dragon Press, 1977).

Schweitzer, Darrell (ed.), *Discovering H.P. Lovecraft* (Starmont House, 1987).

Schweitzer, Darrell, *The Dream-Quest of H.P. Lovecraft* (Borgo Press, 1978).

Shea, J. Vernon, "On the Literary Influences Which Shaped Lovecraft's Works," in S.T. Joshi (ed.), *H.P. Lovecraft: Four Decades of Criticism* (Ohio University Press, 1980).

Shreffler, Philip A., *The H.P. Lovecraft Companion* (Greenwood Press, 1977).

Tierney, Richard L., "The Derleth Mythos" [1972], in Darrell Schweitzer (ed.), *Discovering H.P. Lovecraft* (Starmont House, 1987).

Waugh, Robert H., "*At the Mountains of Madness*: The Subway and the Shoggoth," in Robert H. Waugh, *The Monster in the Mirror: Looking for H.P. Lovecraft* (Hippocampus Press, 2006).

Waugh, Robert H., "Landscapes, Selves, and Others in Lovecraft," in S.T. Joshi and David E. Schultz (eds.), *An Epicure in the Terrible: A Centennial Anthology of Essays in Honor of H.P. Lovecraft* (Fairleigh Dickinson University Press, 1991).

Wetzel, George T., "The Cthulhu Mythos: A Study" [1955, rev. 1971], in S.T. Joshi (ed.), *H.P. Lovecraft: Four Decades of Criticism* (Ohio University Press, 1980).

Wilson, Colin, *The Strength to Dream: Literature and the Imagination* (Gollancz, 1961).

Wilson, Edmund, "Tales of the Marvellous and the Ridiculous" [1945], in S.T. Joshi (ed.), *H.P. Lovecraft: Four Decades of Criticism* (Ohio University Press, 1980).

Index of Lovecraft Tales

"Arthur Jermyn" **15-18,** 23
At the Mountains of Madness v, 3, 18, 20-22, 28, 38, 41, 43, 45, 49, 63, **80-83,** 94, 96
"Beyond the Wall of Sleep" **6-7,** 94
"The Call of Cthulhu" v, 3, 9, 21, 24, 27, 41, 49, 52, **59-62,** 64, 78, 86, 87, 90, 92, 94
The Case of Charles Dexter Ward v, x, 1, 13, 18, 20, 21, 41, 43, 49, **69-71,** 81, 86, 87, 94
"The Cats of Ulthar" v, 9, **18-20,** 22, 34, 42, 63
"Celephaïs" 21, **22-23,** 28, 44, 62, 64, 66
"The Colour Out of Space" i, v, vii, 6, 45, 68, **71-73,** 94
"Cool Air" 30, 50, 53, **57-58**
"Dagon" 1, **2-4,** 11, 21, 23, 28, 38, 45, 46, 62, 86, 92, 98
"The Doom That Came to Sarnath" v, **8-11,** 18, 20-22, 31, 42, 63
The Dream-Quest of Unknown Kadath 2, 7, 21, 28, 33, **65-67,** 68
"The Dreams in the Witch House" v, 2, 7, 21, 38, 43, 55, **86-88**
"The Dunwich Horror" v, 2, 9, 13, 20, **73-78,** 87
"Facts Concerning the Late Arthur Jermyn and His Family" **15-18,** 23
"The Festival" 21, 28, **45-46,** 94
"From Beyond" 22, **24-26,** 33, 43, 68, 86
"The Haunter of the Dark" v, 2, 18, 21, 28, 32, 41, 44, 70, 87, 89, 92, 94, **97-100**
"He" 2, 13, 23, 30, 41, 45, 53, **54-56,** 78, 86
"Herbert West – Reanimator" v, viii, 30, **35-36,** 40, 81
"The Horror at Red Hook" 32, **51-54,** 57
"The Hound" 21, **39-40,** 62, 86
"Hypnos" 13, 21, **37-38,** 62, 86
"Imprisoned With the Pharaohs" **46-49**
"In the Vault" 20, **56-57**

"The Lurking Fear" 2, **40-41,** 62
"The Moon-Bog" 13, **31-32,** 41
"The Music of Erich Zann" v, 9, **36-37,** 42, 43, 49, 54, 86
"The Nameless City" 21, **28-29,** 41, 45, 62
"Nyarlathotep" 14, **23-24,** 54, 78
"The Other Gods" **34**
"The Outsider" v, x, xiv, 12, 18, 31, **32-33,** 67
"Pickman's Model" v, 21, 30, 33, 44, **62-63,** 86
"The Picture in the House" 13, 21, **26-27,** 33, 43, 89
"Polaris" **5-6,** 20, 86
"The Quest of Iranon" **29-30**
"The Rats in the Walls" v, x, 2, 9, 21, 24, 31, 33, **42-44,** 49, 51, 52
"The Shadow Out of Time" v, 2, 3, 5, 7, 18, 23, 41, 43, 45, 50, 86, 92, 94, **95-96**
"The Shadow Over Innsmouth" v, 7, 17, 18, 21, 28, 41, 45, 77, **84-85,** 94
"The Shunned House" v, 21, 43, **49-51,** 62, 69, 89
"The Silver Key" 21, 37, **67-68**
"The Statement of Randolph Carter" **11,** 23, 42
"The Strange High House in the Mist" v, 21, **63-65,** 67, 86
"The Temple" **21-22,** 28, 62
"The Terrible Old Man" **12-13,** 19, 20, 45
"The Thing on the Doorstep" v, 45, 51, **93-95**
"Through the Gates of the Silver Key" **89-92**
"The Tomb" **1-2,** 21, 30, 86, 94, 98
"The Tree" **13-15,** 20
"Under the Pyramids" **46-49**
"The Unnamable" 11, **44-45**
"The Whisperer in Darkness" v, 2, 21, 41, **79-80**
"The White Ship" **7-8,** 21

ABOUT THE AUTHOR

Kenneth Hite is the multiple Origins Award-winning author, co-author, or designer of over 70 roleplaying game books and supplements, including **GURPS Horror, Call of Cthulhu d20,** and most recently, **Trail of Cthulhu** from Pelgrane Press. He has written on the narrative of horror roleplaying in **Nightmares of Mine,** and on the narrative structure of **Call of Cthulhu** in the *Second Person* anthology from MIT Press. His other recent works include the Mythos miscellany *Dubious Shards* and a children's book combining Lovecraft and Sendak, *Where the Deep Ones Are*. His column "Suppressed Transmission" explores the Higher Weirdness in *Pyramid* magazine, and his column "Lost in Lovecraft" explores Lovecraft Country for *Weird Tales*. He lives in Chicago with his wife Sheila, the mandatory Lovecraftian cat, seven thousand or so books, and a sense of adventurous expectancy.